Bagdasarian, Adam
    Forgotten fire

FORGOTTEN
FIRE

A MELANIE KROUPA BOOK

FORGOTTEN
FIRE

Adam Bagdasarian

DORLING KINDERSLEY PUBLISHING, INC.

A Melanie Kroupa Book

Dorling Kindersley Publishing, Inc.
95 Madison Avenue
New York, New York 10016

Visit us on the World Wide Web at http://www.dk.com

Dorling Kindersley books are available at special discounts for bulk purchases for sales promotions or premiums. Special editions, including personalized covers, excerpts of existing guides, and corporate imprints can be created in large quantities for specific needs. For more information, contact Special Markets Dept., Dorling Kindersley Publishing, Inc., 95 Madison Ave., New York, NY 10016; fax: (800) 600-9098.

Library of Congress Cataloging-in-Publication Data
Bagdasarian, Adam.
Forgotten fire / by Adam Bagdasarian.—1st ed.
p. cm.
ISBN 0-7894-2627-7
1. Armenian massacres, 1915–1923—Turkey—Fiction.
2. Armenians—Turkey—History—20th century—Fiction. I. Title.
PS3552.A3355 F6 2000
813'.54—dc21   99-046465

The text of this book is set in 13.5 point Centaur MT.
Map by Debra Ziss

Printed and bound in U.S.A.

4 6 8 10 9 7 5 3

ACKNOWLEDGMENTS

I would like to thank the following people
for their invaluable contributions to this book:

Melanie Kroupa
Alvaro Giraldo
Carol Bagdasarian
Ross Bagdasarian
Priscilla Palmer

Who does now remember the Armenians?

—Adolf Hitler, 1939,
*in support of his argument that
the world would soon forget the
extermination of a people.*

Foreword

Historic Armenia lay at the crossroads between Europe and Asia. Time after time, she was controlled by invaders—Greek, Persian, Roman, and Mongolian. In the first half of the sixteenth century, she fell to the Ottoman Turks. Officially, the Muslim Turks considered the Christian Armenians troublesome inferiors who were beneath the law. Armenians were not allowed to bear arms, found no justice in Muslim courts, and were burdened with taxes so heavy that many lost their possessions, their homes, and their land.

By 1900, one-ninth of the Ottoman Empire's population were Armenians. In the eyes of their Turkish rulers, these two million people were a threat to the government's security. They feared that the Armenians' suffering would attract the attention of European powers, which might intervene and further weaken the crumbling Ottoman Empire. To appease Europe, they promised reforms that they rarely, if ever, implemented.

In 1908, the Young Turk triumvirate—Enver Pasha, Talaat Bey, and Djemal Pasha, leaders of the Committee of Union and Progress—took power, promising an end to the brutality and injustice that had marked Turkish rule for four centuries. They created a democratic parliament that gave Armenians and all other minorities a genuine voice in the government. Constitutional freedoms were assured, old grievances buried, and, for a brief moment, Muslim shook hands with Christian.

This experiment in goodwill barely lasted two years. Members of the Committee of Union and Progress decided that the best way to halt the erosion of Turkish power and remove the threat of European intervention was by "turkifying" or, if necessary, annihilating the non-Muslim minorities and creating a new empire that would extend as far as Russian Transcaucasia and Central Asia. To achieve this, the Young Turk triumvirate gradually withdrew many of the rights they had granted to Christians and returned to a policy of Muslim superiority.

Most Armenians were unaware of the back room machinations that would soon decide their fate. The fortunate ones had never witnessed the Turkish "disciplinary" massacres in cities such as Trebizond and

Sasun and Adana. Some, luckier still, had managed to prosper in Turkey and hold positions of authority. And some, mostly children, believed that their homes, their families, their friends and neighbors were inviolable. This book is based on the true story of one such child.

BOOK ONE

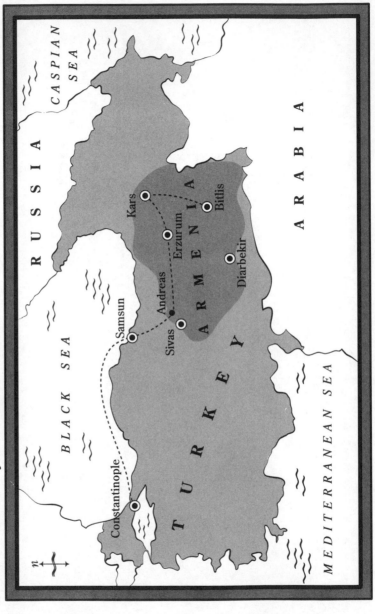

VAHAN'S JOURNEY

RUSSIA

CASPIAN SEA

ARABIA

ARMENIA

Kars

Bitlis

Erzurum

Diarbekir

Andreas

Samsun

Sivas

TURKEY

BLACK SEA

Constantinople

MEDITERRANEAN SEA

Chapter One

My name is Vahan Kenderian. I was born in Bitlis, a province of Turkey, at the base of the Musguneyi Mountains of the East. It was a beautiful city of cobbled streets and horse-drawn wagons, brilliant springs and blighting winters, strolling peddlers and snake charmers. Beyond sun-baked mud-brick houses were fields of tall grass, rolling hills, and orchards of avocado, apricot, olive, and fig trees. Steep valleys of stone climbed sharply to grassy plains and pastures, and higher still to the slopes of snow-capped mountains where every summer evening the sun set in deepening shades of red and blue.

On your way into town, you would walk on crooked sidewalks past houses so close together that a small boy could easily jump from one roof to another. Weaving your way through a tangle of pedestrians, you passed veiled women sitting on stools selling madzoon, and in shop windows you would see merchants dressed in baggy pants and vests, sipping small cups of black coffee. You smelled the lavosh bread from the bakery and stood aside as the cab driver in his two-wheeled horse-drawn cart drove by. Walking home at sunset, you would see the lamplighter carrying a torch in his hand and a ladder on his back. And as darkness fell, all the flat-roofed, tightly packed houses would become one great house where a thousand small lights burned.

As far as an Armenian from Bitlis was concerned, Bitlis was the center of the world: Her mountains were the highest, her soil the most fertile, her women the loveliest, her men the bravest, her leaders the wisest. Of course, not every Armenian from Bitlis was praiseworthy. Some drank, some begged in the street, some swindled their employers, some were vain, careless, licentious, or lazy. But, for the most part, they were a hardworking and honorable people. At least the ones I knew.

In 1915, I was twelve years old, the youngest child of one of the richest and most respected Armenians in Turkey. I was small for my age, stocky and strongly built, with curly brown hair, excellent posture, a firm handshake, and a brisk, determined stride. I walked with the confidence of a boy who has grown up in luxury and knows that he will always be comfortable, always well fed, always warm in winter and cool in summer.

My father was afraid that I lacked character and discipline. And he was right. As far as I was concerned, character and discipline were consolation prizes given to the meek, the unadventurous, and the unlucky. Mrs. Gulbankian needed character because she was a widow and lived alone. Mr. Aberjanian needed discipline because he worked twelve hours a day selling groceries. Most adults, it seemed, needed character and discipline because their lives had long ago ceased to either amuse or fulfill them. "You'll see," they would say to me with knowing smiles, as though disillusion were a law as inevitable as gravity. But I knew better. I knew that time and destiny were my allies, the twin magicians of my fate: Time would transform me into the tallest, strongest man in Bitlis, and destiny would transform me into one of the wealthiest, most admired men in Turkey. I did not know if I would be a lawyer, like my father, or a doctor or a businessman, but I knew that I would be a man of consequence. When I walked down the street, people would say, "There goes Vahan Kenderian," and I would smile or not smile, depending on my mood that day.

Unfortunately, I was an unlikely candidate for greatness—at least by conventional standards: In school I threw wads of paper at my friends Manoosh and Pattoo, spoke out of turn, fell asleep at my desk,

and was generally the first one suspected whenever anything out of the ordinary happened anywhere on the
grounds. Twice I had been sent home for wrestling in
the halls, twelve times for skipping school, once for
falling out of my chair, and once because I had given
one of my teachers "a look."

"What kind of look?" my mother asked me.

"I don't know. I just looked at him."

"*How* did you look at him?"

"I don't know. Like this. Like I'm looking at you."

Father Ossian said I had a poor attitude.

Father Nahnikian said I was looking for attention.

Father Asadourian said I should be disciplined as
often as possible, preferably with a stick.

My father gave me chores to build my character.
When I forgot to do them, he would take me into the
living room, sit me down, look me in the eye, and say,
"What kind of man do you think you are going to
be?" My father had black hair, a black mustache, and
black eyes that could see through anyone or anything.
He was the disciplinarian of the family, who, by exam-
ple, tried to teach his children the laws of honor, in-
tegrity, and self-reliance. He was a man to whom
others often turned for money or support, and he was
always trying, in vain, to draw my consciousness beyond the long white wall that surrounded our property,

to open my eyes to the challenges of the real world. The real world, as far as I could tell, was a terrifying place where half-dead men and women labored, bore children, grew old, grew ill, and died—a drab, inhospitable place where the grim and bitter read to one another from a book of woe. Naturally, I had no interest in that world, and no intention of ever becoming one of its citizens. In *my* real world, cold would always be answered with warmth, hunger with food, thirst with water, loneliness with love. In my real world, there would always be this house I loved, the laughter of brothers and sisters, uncles and cousins. In my real world, I would always belong, and I would always be happy.

Chapter Two

If I close my eyes I can still see my home as it was. I can still climb the green-carpeted stairs, grip the varnished wood banister, and see the same bar of three o'clock sunlight on the top two steps. The landing at the top is covered by a huge rug that my father brought back from Constantinople. At the center of the rug is a blue star, or starlike design, that I wish upon whenever it happens to catch my eye. At the end of the hall is the room I have shared with my brother Sisak from the time I was old enough to sleep in a bed. On my little desk by the window I see the paperweight my father gave me, the coin bank Sisak gave me, the lamp I study by. I see Sisak's bed at a right angle to mine, our heads nearly touching: "Good night, Vahan." "Good night, Sisak."

Someone, perhaps Uncle Mumpreh, is playing the piano downstairs. I hear the front door open and close and Karnig, our houseman, greeting my mother. My sister Oskina is outside helping Sisak and my brother

Tavel with their chores. My sister Armenouhi is braiding her hair, preparing to meet one of the hundred suitors who come daily to our house to be near her, and my oldest brother, Diran, the pride of the family, is in his room, studying the books that will help him someday become a great lawyer. They are all safe inside me, and there will never be a war, and the leaders of Turkey will remain in their offices, forever plotting a murder more terrible than any the new century has seen.

I didn't know very much about the Turks in 1915. I knew that we were taught their language in school; I knew that we went to different churches, but I did not know that we were enemies. Turkish officials, smiling and polite, visited our house often to consult with my father. They shook my hand and said that they were pleased to meet me. They admired our home in the most flattering language and brought my mother small gifts as tokens of their respect for my father.

There were not very many Turks in Bitlis in those days, but those I encountered were never unfriendly in any way, and the Turkish merchants seemed no different than their Armenian counterparts. I knew, of course, that Turkey had once been called Armenia, but as far as I could tell, not much besides the name had changed. I was sure that the streets of Bitlis had been no lovelier then, that the fruit from the trees had been no sweeter, the sky no clearer or bluer. Only the name was different.

I had heard something about a Turkish massacre of Armenians several years before, in Adana, but I was sure it was something else—a war of some kind, and not murder, uniformed Turks battling uniformed Armenians. I was not told any details (I was *never* told any details), so it was only my father shaking his head, the dinner table quiet, Uncle Mumpreh talking urgently and quietly to my grandmother. "We can't trust them," I remember him saying, referring to the Turks. "We can't *ever* trust them." But I knew he could not be talking about *our* Turks—not the polite men who came to our house, not the merchants who greeted me when I went to their stores to buy bread, or the families I saw coming out of the mosques, where they prayed as we prayed.

But in 1915, after Turkey entered World War I as an ally of Germany and an enemy of Russia, after many of my uncles and cousins went away to fight for the Turkish army, and the fires of war screened the Armenians from the eyes of our European protectors, I would learn that some of the Turks of Adana were also the Turks of Bitlis.

Chapter Three

Early in the spring of 1915, two gendarmes came to see my father. They told him that he was wanted at the government building. "Official business," they said.

I did not understand. Government officials often came to the house, but always in suits and usually to ask my father's advice. But these were policemen. Had my father broken the law, or did the government simply want to consult with him? I looked at my mother to see if she understood. She was staring at my father as though he were ill and could not be nursed back to health.

"Sarkis," she said.

"It's nothing," my father said, and kissed her. Then, with a surprisingly tender smile, he patted my shoulder and went away with the gendarmes.

At dinner that night, my grandmother, Toumia, the wisest and most respected voice in our family, assured my mother that my father would be back tomorrow. "They only want to talk to him," she said.

"He knows more about running this city than they do," Uncle Mumpreh said. My mother nodded and agreed. Everyone agreed.

But my father did not return the next day, or the day after that. Usually I was relieved when he was away because it meant that I could relax a little and not worry about whether or not I had done my chores half- or wholeheartedly or picked up my feet when I walked or accidentally sighed when I returned home from school. (Sighing, he believed, was a prelude to whining and should be avoided by all but the very old, the very ill, or the very weary. Everyone else, especially his children and most especially his *male* children, should face life with strength and vitality.) But this time was different. This time I sensed that something might be wrong, and every time I'd start to enjoy my freedom, I'd see my father being led away by the gendarmes.

In the outside world I thought of myself as a grown man, independent of my family, but in my own home I was merely a twelve-year-old boy who had been frightened by my father's absence. So I did what I usually did when I was afraid: I went to my mother's room.

My mother had hazel eyes, brown hair, and a smile as tender and reassuring as a child could want. Though she was herself a worrier, she was an unfailing antidote for worry in others and was as openhanded with her counsel as she was openhearted with her love. I wanted her to tell me that my father was safe and that I was foolish to be afraid. I wanted her to smile her most reassuring smile and convince me that there was nothing to fear.

When I entered, she looked up from the book she was reading as though she had been waiting for me. She knew why I was there and what I needed, and as I sat near her on my father's side of the bed, all my questions seemed smaller and less urgent and I was relieved to be a child again. For a moment I did not know what to ask first or how to ask it. But my mother already knew the questions.

"You're worried about Father?" she said.

I nodded.

She took my hand. "Father is fine," she said. "He had to go away."

"To Paris?" Paris was where my father usually went on business. Sometimes London or Constantinople.

"Yes," my mother said.

"For how long?"

She smiled. "We'll see. Not very long, I think."

I still didn't know why the gendarmes had come for him, but I was afraid to ask her a question that I knew she couldn't answer.

"Are *you* worried?" I asked.

My mother shook her head. "And I don't want you to worry either. All right?"

I nodded.

"I love you very much," she said. "Do you know that?"

"Yes," I said.

"Do you feel better?"

I did. And I left her room feeling better, even though I knew that everything she had told me about my father was a lie.

Things began to happen very quickly after that. The next day I saw six men being led away by three gendarmes. The shirts of two of the men were ripped and bloody, and their faces were cut and bruised. One of the men was the father of my friend Aram Khatisian, an engineer of great renown.

A short time later, the stores closed. First the bakery, then the cobbler's, then the butcher shop. Oskina and Armenouhi had heard screams coming from the prison. Diran had heard gunshots coming from the center of town. Tavel had heard that the homes of two Armenian families had been set on fire and burned to the ground. And then my mother took me out of school, and I was told not to leave the house.

There was no question now that this was our

Adana, and between us all, unspoken, was the fear that it might somehow reach us, that it might already have reached my father. We made a point of never mentioning him, fearing, I suppose, that his life hung by a thread and that any expression of uncertainty on our part would condemn him to death. I awoke every morning certain that the worst was over, but by the end of the day there was always more. Now they were searching the homes of Armenians for guns. Now they were ransacking our churches and accusing our priests of preaching sedition. Some Armenians were fighting back, futilely, in homes that were set on fire, some died barricaded behind mud walls. Two or three times a day I would open our front door and listen for the sound of gunfire and, hearing nothing, try to believe that the fighting was over. I sniffed the air for the smoke of burning houses and, smelling nothing, tried to believe that the world was safe again.

Two days after I was taken out of school, Uncle Mumpreh was gone. "To prison," Sisak told me. "They came for him early this morning."

"Why?"

"They claim he's a revolutionary," my brother said.

Chapter Four

Uncle Mumpreh, my father's younger brother, was a jovial, red-faced comedian who entered our front door every evening with a new joke, a piece of candy for me, and the faint odor of pipe smoke and raki and spice cologne. Because he was the black sheep of his family, as I was in mine, we had a special rapport, a secret code of winks and half smiles that acknowledged our status as good-hearted rogues destined to float contentedly on our backs through life. Though a gifted student, he had got only as far as his second year in medical school before deciding that he would prefer to heal incidentally rather than exclusively. Still, he always carried the black bag of a doctor and often applied the contents of that bag, free of charge, toward the good health of those who could not afford the services of a real doctor—setting broken bones, applying tourniquets, banishing coughs and fevers with skill, compassion, and humor.

This was the man whom the gendarmes had

accused of being a revolutionary, and, in my eyes, his arrest transformed our fortress into something like a birdcage where all the locks and bolts and latches were on the wrong side of the door and the eyes of giants might appear in any window. I knew then that all the rumors were true, all the screams were real.

And it was only the beginning.

From the province of Van came hundreds of Armenian women and children whose husbands and fathers had been killed and whose villages had been destroyed, not by the Russian army, but by the Turkish army— our own army. We heard many stories about a barbarian named Selim Bey, the governor of Van, who had murdered Armenians by the thousands. We heard that the men of our town, the men we saw every day, our friends, our neighbors, had all been shot on the way to Diarbekir.

Mariam, our cook, returned to Van to see what had happened to her family. The next day Karnig, our houseman, disappeared, and no one would tell me where or why. That night I went to Oskina's room and asked her what had happened to him.

Oskina was my older sister, and though we did our best, in a good-natured way, to make each other's lives as miserable as possible, she was as protective of my well-being as any parent would be. She had bathed me until I was six years old, came to my room three or four times a day when I was sick, and was forever tucking in my shirt or wiping something off my chin with her handkerchief. Though she was a high-spirited tomboy whom everyone agreed should be a little more docile in the company of young men ("You have your whole life to show a man who you are," my grandmother once told her with a smile. "Let him dream for a while."), she had an adult air of maturity about her that often drew me to her room late at night when I needed advice or comfort and all the bedroom doors were closed. For this reason I went to her room and asked her what had happened to Karnig.

"I don't know," she said, and I knew she was lying.

"Please tell me," I said, knowing that she prized honesty above all other virtues and could not lie to me for long.

Oskina looked doubtful. Finally, however, she revealed that Karnig had hanged himself when he learned that his father and mother and two brothers had been killed in Van.

I did not want to ask the next question, but if Karnig was dead, if Karnig could hang himself and really be dead . . .

"Is Father dead?"

"They say that all the men were shot on the way to Diarbekir," Oskina said, very quietly.

I don't know why, but I smiled. Maybe because if I cried, then my father would really be dead, or maybe because I wanted to reduce his death to something as small as a smile. Oskina smiled, too, but hers was a sad smile, and full of understanding. "We must be very strong now," she said.

A few mornings later I was awakened by the sound of voices below my bedroom window. I ran to the window, opened it, and saw a river of people moving past our house—eight or nine hundred of them, all Armenian, with soldiers and gendarmes on either side. I saw women with babies on their backs, old men carrying blankets and bundles of food, brothers and sisters holding each other's hands. Some of the women were crying or calling out for help, but there was no one to help them. I tried to pick out a face I knew from the crowd, but I was too far away and there were too many faces. Finally, afraid to look any longer, I ran to Diran's room, where I saw him and Sisak looking out the window at the same sight.

At dinner that night we all discussed what we had seen and what it meant and what we should do, as though we still had control over our lives. Diran and

Tavel said that we should get guns to protect ourselves. Sisak argued that nothing could save us from an army of soldiers and gendarmes and we should try to escape. My grandmother insisted that we would not be harmed because my father was an influential man with many friends in the government.

"You see what his friends have done for him," Oskina said.

"That's enough!" my mother said. And Oskina apologized for her disrespect.

Armenouhi excused herself from the table and ran upstairs.

"No more talk about this now," my mother said.

"We *have* to talk about it," Diran answered.

"No more," my grandmother said, and the table was silenced.

The next day Uncle Mumpreh was brought home by two gendarmes. We all embraced him, and my mother and grandmother cried. I stood a little behind them, staring at a man I hardly recognized. This man, the man the gendarmes had returned to us, was haggard and gaunt, and there were marks that looked like burns on his face and hands.

He looked around the room as though he had awakened from a dream and was not quite sure where he was. He said he was thirsty and asked for water. He drank two glasses, then spoke privately with my mother and my grandmother and Diran. What he told them, I don't know, but later that day he filled three small bags with poison and told the women to hang the bags around their necks.

"If there is any trouble," he said, "take the poison and it will all be over."

No one asked him what kind of trouble could be worse than death. They all seemed to know.

The next morning he was gone. No one knew where, and I do not think anyone knew why. Perhaps he feared that the gendarmes would come back for him or that his presence in the house was a danger to us all.

That night I lay in bed looking at the night outside my window. Sisak was asleep in the bed next to mine, and I listened to the sound of his breathing. He was three years older than I, my friend, playmate, guide, and protector, but now, listening to him sleep, I realized how vulnerable he was, how vulnerable we all were. I sat up and watched him. I heard our laughter on hundreds of nights past and my father's voice cautioning us to go to sleep. I saw us lying in our beds, both sick with the same sore throat, consoled by the fact that we were together.

"We must be very strong now," Oskina had said,

---

but I was afraid, afraid of this moment and of the knock on the door that meant that we, too, would have to leave the city. I was afraid of the trouble that would make my mother and my sisters have to take the poison. I wondered if my mother was asleep. I wished I could go to her room and tell her I was afraid. But somehow I knew that I couldn't. I knew that a part of her had gone away with my father, and that her room was no longer a place I belonged. I closed my eyes and saw my father dead on the road to Diarbekir. I heard the shot that killed him, saw him fall to the ground. I made myself see this again and again so that I would know that he was really dead and stop waiting for him to come home.

Chapter Five

I did not know when I opened my eyes the next morning that it was the last day of my childhood. The day seemed no more ominous than the one before; my heart was no heavier, my fears no greater. As I walked down the stairs to the kitchen, I had no premonition that my family and I were about to share our last meal together.

I do not remember that meal very well. I am sure that Diran, conscious of his role as the oldest son and being a natural leader and optimist, said something to raise our spirits and give us hope. And I am sure that Tavel, his shadow and best friend, agreed and added some encouragement of his own. If I had known what lay ahead that morning, I would have cherished every word my brothers spoke, the sound of their voices, the sight of them sitting across from me. I would have told them that I loved them with all my heart and that I would never forget them for as long as I lived.

As it was, I was probably lost in my own thoughts when Sisak ran into the kitchen and told us that Turkish soldiers had surrounded our house.

I ran to the window and counted seven soldiers, each with a rifle. Four of them started toward the back door as Armenouhi ran into the kitchen. Diran opened the door and the soldiers fired. The bullets splintered the door and shattered the glass. There were two more shots and then the soldiers were in our kitchen, pushing us against the wall, asking us if there was anyone else in the house.

"No," my mother said.

"No servants?"

"Our servants are gone."

"Are you hiding anyone? Neighbors or friends?"

"No."

"If anyone is found, all of you will be shot and this house will be burned to the ground. Are you hiding anyone?"

"No," my mother said.

"Take them outside."

Two soldiers took us to the garden in front of our house where we stood together under a perfect spring sky.

No one said a word. Armenouhi was crying softly,

and my grandmother was stroking her hair and kissing the side of her head. Diran was holding my mother's hand, and Tavel was standing close to him, almost leaning against him. Oskina stood beside Tavel, her face pallid and drawn in the sunlight. I was standing next to Sisak, staring at the soldiers who were guarding us, then at their rifles. I had never really believed that we could die, and now that possibility was perhaps only five or ten minutes away. There would be eight shots, and somewhere on the other side of the wall a few heads would turn and someone would make a joke about there being eight less Armenians in Bitlis.

My body was shaking as though I had caught a chill, and I felt Sisak take my wrist and hold it tightly. I had read books about soldiers, adventurers, and kings, men who faced death with a smile and even managed to say something memorable before they died. Secretly, I had always thought that I was one of them, that given the opportunity I, too, could face death with a wink or a shrug or a smile. And now I knew that I was not brave, that my fear of death was so strong that I could not control my own body.

And then the other soldiers returned. The one who had questioned my mother in the kitchen stood before her now, appraising her, it seemed, with all the contempt and self-importance of a born bully.

"Where is Mumpreh Kenderian?" he demanded.

"I don't know," my mother said. "He left yesterday morning."

"You are his sister?"

"His sister-in-law."

"And he did not tell his sister-in-law where he was going?"

"He left before anyone was awake. I didn't know he was leaving," my mother said. Her voice was small and hollow, like the voice of a child.

"No one knew he was leaving," Diran said, bravely trying to draw attention away from our mother.

The soldier turned to him. "How old are you?"

"Nineteen."

He pointed at Tavel. "And you?"

"Seventeen," Tavel said.

The soldier nodded and looked at my mother. "You may all go inside. If Mumpreh Kenderian returns you will tell us?"

"Yes," my mother said. "Thank you."

Our guards lowered their rifles and began to walk away. We were no longer prisoners.

As I took my first step toward the front door, my

---

legs gave and I nearly fell to my knees. For the first time I noticed that the door was open and that there were bullet holes around the keyhole and the brass handle.

I heard some kind of commotion behind me, and when I turned, I saw two soldiers leading Diran and Tavel to the garden wall. Two other soldiers were standing a few yards away, their rifles pointed at my brothers.

"What are you doing?" my mother said to one of them, but he didn't answer. "They didn't do anything!" my mother shouted. "They don't know anything!" She started to run to my brothers, and another soldier grabbed her arm. "They didn't do anything!" she cried. But the soldiers had already raised their rifles, had already aimed.

Tavel had slipped halfway down the wall when the shots exploded, blowing his body back against the wall. And then he and Diran were on their sides, and the white wall was red and blood leaked from Diran's head, from Tavel's chest and head, and puddled beneath them. Sisak started toward the bodies. Armenouhi dropped to her knees, and my mother screamed and screamed.

The soldier who had questioned my mother drew his pistol, walked to the bodies, pressed the mouth of the gun against each skull, fired, put the gun in his holster, and walked away.

Sisak and I dug the graves in the grass behind the house. We wrapped our brothers in blankets and lowered them into the earth. My grandmother read from the Bible, and Oskina and Armenouhi planted a wood cross at the head of each grave.

Day and night my mother stared out the window at the garden, reliving the murder of her sons. Overnight, it seemed, her brown hair turned white, and her face had grown old. The house was silent, and every window seemed to look out on the garden where Diran and Tavel had been shot.

My grandmother knitted in her chair by the toneer in the living room. Oskina began wearing my father's shirts, and every evening after dinner Sisak could be found sitting in the grass beside Diran's and Tavel's graves. I moved through each day as though I was myself, yet I was not myself. I might have died with Diran and Tavel, or I might be screaming in prison or hanging from Karnig's noose, but I was no longer in our house or even inside myself. Armenouhi rarely left her bedroom. More than any of us, she had been undone by the events of the last four weeks, and now she could not sleep and ate very little and often held herself as though she were cold. She was afraid that the soldiers would return, afraid of what they would do to her. We assured her that she was safe, that they had already searched the house and had no reason to return. But a week later they did.

We were all taken to the garden, where the same two soldiers stood before us with the same rifles and the same expressionless faces. I was standing between my mother and Sisak, waiting for the other soldiers to return and take my brother and me to the wall. Sisak was as still as a statue, holding my hand. My mother held my other hand, half shielding me with her body. I wanted to be a man for her, to press her hand to my lips and tell her that I was not afraid to die. But I could not move or speak or even look at her.

Finally, the soldier who had questioned my mother the first time questioned her again. This time, however, I barely heard the words because this time I knew that I was going to die.

After all the questions had been asked and answered, the soldier looked at Armenouhi admiringly, as though seeing her for the first time. He took a step toward her, and she lowered her eyes, then her head. Even from a distance of ten feet, I could see that she was trembling. The soldier turned to my mother. "You will all come with us," he said.

"Where are you taking us?" Oskina said, as though she were addressing a cab driver who had purposely taken a wrong turn. Only Oskina, who had inherited my father's brave heart and level gaze, could have gotten away with such effrontery.

The soldier shot a glance at her, but Oskina just stared at him.

"Goryan's Inn," he said.

And with that, the other soldiers became a wall, pushing us out of our garden, away from our home. I did not know at the time that I was leaving my house forever. I only knew that I was alive, and for a moment I was happy. But as I walked past the open gate and the soldiers mounted their horses, I looked up the street and my heart fell.

Chapter Six

I had not set foot beyond our garden wall in six weeks and was not prepared for what I saw. The street was deserted as far as the eye could see, and there was a silence I had never heard before on any street. Through open windows and half-open doors there was no sign of life, only gates waiting to be closed, walkways waiting to be swept.

Everyone was gone—Mr. and Mrs. Papazian, Arshak, Mr. Danubian, and Mrs. Gulbankian. I had seen them below my bedroom window; I had heard them calling for help, and now we were walking up the silence of our street past the ghosts of their houses, the ghosts of their gardens.

It was Wednesday, bazaar day, but all the shops were closed. The windows of several stores were broken, and the streets were dirty with old newspapers, rotted fruit, broken glass, and stains that could only be blood. Strangely, I wondered who would light the streetlamps tonight, and somehow all those unlit lamps and the lamplighters who were not there to light them were the most hopeless sight of all. I wondered where they were—the lamplighters, the blacksmith, my teachers and classmates. Whose blood had stained the streets?

As we neared the road that led out of the city, I saw the collapsed wall of the dry goods store, and beneath the wall something brown and dry like branches. When I realized that the branches were arms and legs, I looked away.

"Your neighbors?" one of the soldiers said, and the other soldiers laughed.

And then we were out of the city and walking on dirt toward Diarbekir. To our left was a farm, green and deserted, the horses stolen, the farmhouse empty or inhabited by Turks. Somehow the world I had known had disappeared, and in its place was this dirt road before me and the threat of Goryan's Inn. My grandmother, as though sensing my fears, took my hand in hers. I had forgotten that I was not alone, and now, holding the softness and familiarity of her hand, I almost felt safe again. I prayed silently, asking God to protect my family and to please walk beside each of us.

In the distance I saw Goryan's Inn.

All the windows were boarded, and there were iron strips running lengthwise across the boards. There was a handful of soldiers sitting or standing by the posts where their horses were tied, and we walked past them to the open door.

When we entered the lobby, I saw that the space behind the counter where Mr. Goryan might once have stood was deserted and that there were no keys hanging from any of the hooks. The lobby was dark, unlit by either lamps or sunlight, and there were cigarette butts on the floor and a stale smell of smoke in the air. Still, I tried to reassure myself, it was a lobby, not a prison, and the steep stairs we climbed would certainly lead to a row of rooms better than any jail cell.

At the top of the stairway was a dark, sour-smelling hall of closed doors. I did not know what the smell was, and I did not want to know. I wanted to go home; I wanted to wake up sweating and frightened in the middle of the night and see Sisak sound asleep in the bed next to mine.

A soldier who had been standing at the end of the hall came forward, drawing a key from his pocket. He inserted the key into the lock of one of the doors and pressed down on the handle. As the door opened, the sour smell became a stench so strong that I had to breathe through my mouth.

Looking into the room, I saw only darkness at first. Then I heard a sound and a part of the floor moved, and I realized it was a floor of bodies.

"Get in!"

A hand shoved me hard from behind, and I lurched into the room, bumping into Armenouhi as the door slammed shut behind us. The room was black. As my eyes adjusted to the darkness, I saw that there were two windows, each barred on the inside, boarded on the outside. There was a crack of sunlight where the two boards met, and by that light I could gradually make out the fifty or sixty bodies—some on their backs, some on their sides, their feet bare, their clothes turning to rags. Whatever pretense of hope or optimism remained inside me had by now completely disappeared, and I reached in the dark for the first hand I found and held it tightly, not knowing or caring whose hand it was.

We began to walk across the room, stepping as carefully as we could over and around the other prisoners, and as we did I heard the stirring of limbs and torsos pressing upon one another to make a path for us.

We found our way to a corner of the room and sat down. The room was warm, and the air was heavy and moist and hard to breathe. I looked about myself uncomprehendingly, for it was a place too awful to be real.

"Who are you?" a voice beside us said, a woman's voice, dry and weary.

"Meera Kenderian," my mother said.

"From Bitlis?"

"Yes."

"Do you have any food?"

"No," my mother said.

"Water?"

"We have no water. I'm sorry." I could see the woman now, a tired lined face as moist as clay.

"Don't they feed you?" Sisak asked.

"I haven't eaten for four days."

"They want us to die," said another voice from another part of the room. "They don't want Armenians in their country."

"They're devils," said still another.

"Do you have daughters?" asked the woman beside us. "I cannot see very well."

"Yes," my mother said. "Two daughters."

The woman was silent for a moment. "Protect them," she whispered. "At night the soldiers come."

I did not know at the time exactly what the woman meant, but if words could cast a shadow, then I saw it on my sisters' faces and felt the chill of it on my skin.

Hours passed. I listened to moans more despairing than any sounds I had ever heard and watched the sliver of light between the boards—the light of the world,

---

of homes and cities where children still went to school and families were still safe. As that world faded, my eyes grew heavy and I slept. When I awoke, the light was gone, replaced by a pale line of light beneath the door. I wiped my forehead, and it was wet. My shirt was wet with perspiration, and I could feel the smell of the room on my skin and in my mouth. For the first time in my life, I was hungry and there was no food, I was thirsty and there was no water. I knew then as I had not known before that the room was real and that my home and my room and my bed had been a dream.

Armenouhi was crying softly in the darkness. Oskina held her and told her not to be afraid. "No one is coming for us," she said.

"No one will hurt you, Armenouhi," my mother said. But Armenouhi could not stop crying, and her face, once so beautiful, with features as fine and delicate as an engraving, was almost unrecognizable now.

We all sat together in silence for what seemed like hours.

When we heard the footsteps, Sisak inched closer to me so that our sisters were completely hidden behind us. We heard a key in the lock, then the bolt retract. The door opened, and I saw a dark figure, backlit by the hall light, holding a lamp in his hand.

He had no face, no eyes or mouth, but was only a broad shadow stepping into the dark room, looking down at the bowed heads before him.

He held the lamp before one face, then passed on to another, and another. As he neared the middle of the room, I heard Armenouhi pressing herself into the corner, the floor creaking beneath her. There was no other sound, and every eye in the room was on the soldier, waiting to see whom he would choose.

With his free hand he raised the head of a girl and held the lamp to her face. I could see her profile in the light, and the green collar of her dress. When he reached down and pulled her to her feet, the girl did not scream or even try to resist. Perhaps she had screamed before; perhaps she had already tried to resist. Head bowed, she went away with the soldier. I followed the sound of footsteps down the hall, down the stairs, to silence.

"He's gone," my mother said, and Oskina, then Armenouhi, sat up.

"You see," someone whispered. "You see what they do?"

I didn't. Not really. But I looked behind me at my sisters, and they saw it. My mother saw it.

A few minutes later, another soldier entered the room and pulled another girl to her feet. But this girl screamed, and this girl's mother begged the soldier not to take her daughter. "I will give you everything I have," she said. "I have a home and jewelry. I have jewelry. As much as you want. Please don't take her. Please don't take her from me."

But the soldier had made his choice, and he pulled the girl out the door. I heard her screams after the door had been closed and locked. I heard her mother cry in the dark.

In a dead voice my mother said, "He's gone," but this time only Oskina sat up. Armenouhi was lying on her side, holding her stomach as though she were ill. My grandmother asked her what was wrong, but Armenouhi did not answer.

"Are you sick, Armenouhi?" my mother said, bending over her.

Armenouhi shook her head, and then she began to moan, and I saw the bag of poison beside her on the floor. I reached for the bag and my mother grabbed it and looked inside.

"Did you take this?" she said. "Did you take this, Armenouhi?"

Armenouhi did not answer; she could not speak.

"Did you take this, Armenouhi? Oh, God! Oh, God!"

Armenouhi was facing the wall now, moaning and clutching her stomach, clawing at her stomach and screaming as though she were on fire. She stood up, then fell to the floor, screaming and clawing at her chest and stomach. Sisak tried to hold her, but the pain made her impossible to hold. The pain contorted her body and twisted it like a puppet on the floor. I watched her dumbly, unable to move or to speak. I told myself that she would not die, that she had not taken enough poison to die. She would suffer a little longer and then she would rest, she would sleep. She was sick, and she would get well again; she was in pain, and the pain would pass; she would scream, and the screaming would end.

But when she finally stopped screaming and her body was still, she was dead.

The next morning, a soldier threw her body over his shoulder like a sack of flour and carried her out of the room. In the darkness I shivered, though I was not cold, and cried until my body ached.

The day, which was only a sliver of light, passed without food or water. On the other side of the bars there was food, on the other side of the boards there was water, but the boards could not be broken and the bars could not be bent. As the light began to fade, grief turned to weariness, weariness to despair, despair to sleep. I awoke in wet pants, sucking my tongue for moisture, no longer certain whether the light through the boards was the beginning or the end of the day.

As time passed, I began to know my fellow prisoners by their moans and whispers, and I began to know death by the absence of those sounds. In dreams I heard a soldier say, "That one's dead," and a body being dragged from the room. And as the line dividing sleep and wakefulness began to blur and I felt the pull of death in my dreams, I heard a soldier say, "That one's dead," and when I opened my eyes, I saw that the woman who had spoken to us our first day was gone.

Chapter Seven

"**G**et up!"

The room was warm now and the terrible smell was gone, and the rifle was a finger poking my shoulder.

"All of you! Get up!"

And then I truly awoke and began to know where I was, and the early-morning cold returned, crisp and dead and odorless. (I had wondered for days where the odor was, not realizing that I had become a part of it.)

I tried to stand, but I couldn't. My legs were numb and my knees so stiff that I could not unbend them even an inch without pain. Slowly, very slowly, I made it to my feet, my legs actually wobbling with the effort, and watched the soldiers pull the other prisoners to their feet until only the dead were left lying on the floor.

We were herded down the stairs, through the lobby, and into a blinding white morning. Beyond a mist of trees, a warm sun was rising over a brilliant white field. My hands in the sunlight looked small and pale—the hands of a sick child. My arms belonged to that same child, and the faces of my family were almost unrecognizable, the faces of ghosts and mourners. My sister Oskina was a wraith with great black eyes, tangled brown hair, and lips as thirsty as my own. My mother was an old woman with white hair and withered white arms. Only my grandmother was unchanged. Her back was still straight, her eyes clear and proud.

I looked at Sisak, a smaller and grayer Sisak who made my heart ache, and he smiled. We were both squinting like moles because the sun seemed intensely bright, even though it had barely risen. I wanted to ask him or my mother or my grandmother if there was a chance we might be fed or even allowed to go home, but I didn't because I was afraid that all the answers might be no. So I squinted and filled my lungs with fresh air and marveled at the feebleness of my limbs.

We were soon joined by other Armenians from other rooms. There were at least two hundred of them, with faces and bodies that could not be real. Like us, they squinted and shielded their eyes from the morning light. We stood together, dazed and blinded, as dumb and unresisting as cattle.

With the butts of their rifles, the soldiers began to prod us toward the dirt road in front of the inn. Oskina turned and glared at a soldier who had pushed her from behind. The soldier showed her the barrel of his rifle, but my sister did not look away; my mother had to pull her away.

There were seven soldiers on either side of us now, two in front, and two in back. One of them gave the command to walk, and we walked, away from our homes, toward Diarbekir. As we passed the inn I looked to my right and saw a pile of bodies on a hill of manure. There must have been thirty or forty of them, and among them, near the top, I saw a blue dress, Armenouhi's dress, her legs and shoes, and then the back of her head, her brown hair. I swallowed then, maybe to keep from crying or calling to her or running to her. More than anything I did not want to leave her behind, yet I kept walking, mechanically, not knowing how I walked, but moving forward just the same, as though my upper and lower body were two separate species—a man and the animal that the man was riding. I looked over my shoulder at her and did not look away until I couldn't see her anymore.

Behind me I heard voices pleading for water, for mercy. And then I heard the crack of a whip and a cry that did not sound human. Someone had fallen or someone had fainted, but I did not look back. All I could do was walk, and keep walking, and not faint, and not fall back, and not think about where we were

---

walking or what would happen to us there. "There" did not exist. "There" was the other side of the world, the bottom of the ocean. I didn't care about "there," only about putting one foot in front of the other.

I told myself that I was only walking to school. I was only walking to town. I was walking from my home to the home of my friend Manoosh, past Manoosh's house to Pattoo's house, past Pattoo's house to the mountains, to a certain stream, beyond the stream to a clearing where I used to camp. I was only walking in the mountains as I had a hundred times before. Diran, my cousin Mesok, Sisak, and I would spend the day near a stream and eat chocolate and dried apricots for lunch. I would walk upstream and sit naked in the hollow of a boulder, the water washing over my legs.

I felt the sun searing the side of my face, and I tasted the dust rising off the road. I looked up and saw the sun halfway up the sky, rising over a colorless and unfamiliar field. I saw the long trail of prisoners ahead, and the longer road before them.

My mother stumbled, and Sisak put his arm around her waist to support her. My grandmother began to pray. She took my hand, and I closed my eyes and listened. I tried to swallow, but my mouth was too dry. I closed my eyes and prayed for water. I saw streams of clear, sweet water washing over the rocks, into my hands, over my body. And then I felt myself begin to sink inside, and I opened my eyes. "Why don't they kill us now?" I heard someone say.

Hours later, the soldiers told us to stop. We were somewhere in the woods, the air cooler now and smelling of a recent rain. The red earth was moist, almost spongy underfoot, darker and wetter in the places where the trees blocked the sun. To our left the road sloped ten feet to dirt and rocks, and to our right, encircled by oak trees, was a beautiful, bubbling spring. Some of the prisoners had seen it earlier than others, and a whispered report floated up and down the line: "water" . . . "water" . . . I could almost taste it myself, and my heart lifted—but only for a moment. With the barrels and butts of their rifles, the soldiers ordered us back to the opposite side of the road. Only *they* would drink from the spring.

We did as we were told, slowly, in one staggering body, and sat, or, rather, collapsed to the ground. I dug my fingers into the wet soil as if they were roots that could absorb water, and watched the soldiers walk to the spring in shifts, cup the cool water in their hands, and drink and drink until their faces were flushed and their bellies were full. I watched them splash their faces with the spring water and rinse out their mouths and fill the leather pouches they carried. I watched the wasted water drip from their chins and mustaches, and I longed to be a soldier who could drink from a spring, or a pair of hands or a mustache that was wet with spring water.

"Don't look," my grandmother said.

I pretended not to hear her.

"Don't look, Vahan," she said, taking my chin and turning my head toward her.

"Why?"

"First you look, then you beg," she said. "And you are not a beggar."

"I'm thirsty," I said. But she knew that; she was thirsty, too.

I closed my eyes and sucked the blood from my cracked lips as though it were water. My head fell forward, and I felt myself begin to slip away.

Then the command to walk was given. Those who could not go on were shot or run through with bayonets. And the march began again.

We had not walked very far before we began to see the debris from earlier marches—blankets and comforters and household utensils, the hastily gathered possessions of those who had come before us. When I saw the first body, I looked away. Then, thinking that it might be my father, I looked. It was a woman, naked, her left breast bloody where the bayonet had entered. And then I saw another body, and another. There were hundreds of them on the road and alongside the road where grass and wildflowers grew. I do not know how many more we passed. I did not want to know or see or smell. I breathed through my mouth and listened to my grandmother pray for the dead. But her voice was no longer strong, and her words were not clear. There was dirt in the deep lines of her face, on her lips and eyelids. I took her hand and squeezed gently and felt a faint reply.

When the sun barely touched the tops of the trees, we were led off the road to a flat place by the River Tigris. It was the same river Sisak and Oskina and I had swum in the year before, and now it was congested with thousands of corpses. They were floating face up, face down, naked and clothed, the rust-colored water washing over and around them.

Perhaps I knew then that we were going to die, that we had been brought here to die and that before the sun set there would be two hundred more bodies floating in that river. But by then I was so weary and so thirsty that all I saw was water, and I did not care what color the water was or what was floating in it.

The soldiers spread out, and it was understood that

those who wished to drink could do so. I started toward the river, but my mother stopped me. "It's poisoned," she said. But my grandmother didn't care. Already she was walking with sixty or seventy others. I watched as she kneeled, cupped the water in her hands, and drank. Her white hair was in a bun, and her shawl hung loosely over her back and shoulders.

I thought nothing of the soldier who was standing beside her. Only when he raised his hand over his head did I see the rock, and then it was too late. My grandmother lay flat on the bank, her head in the water. And then I heard gunfire, saw the soldiers firing on the prisoners by the river, saw the bodies flatten out or lurch forward. I dropped to the ground and covered my head with my hands, the world exploding around me.

Chapter Eight

Maybe fifty had been killed, and each lay where he had fallen. The bank of the river was strewn with the dead and dying, and we watched the soldiers walk among them, raise their bayonets, and thrust deep into the exposed necks and chests and bellies as though they were made of cloth and sawdust.

My grandmother lay on the bank with her face in the water. There was no one to dig a grave for her or to cover her body with even a handful of dirt. I could still feel her hand holding mine; I could still see her walking to the river, yet I was numb to her death.

It was harder for me to look at my mother because she was not dead. It was harder for me to look at her and know that her suffering was not over and that there was nothing I could do to stop it, nothing I could say that would bring back her brown hair or the light and color in her eyes.

As the sun set behind the mountains, the soldiers began to walk among us. They pulled certain boys to their feet, took them to the river, and shot them in cold blood. Four boys were killed in this way, boys no older than Sisak, no older than I. We heard the shots, saw the bodies fall, and it was all a part of the same dream—the dream of morning outside the inn, and now the dream of dusk, of a river disappearing into darkness. After the last shot, we sat in silence, each of us gazing at the river, at nothing at all. A cold wind was blowing off the mountains.

"When it gets dark," my mother said to Sisak, "I want you and Vahan to run away."

Sisak and I started to protest, though we knew, as my mother did, that it was the males that the Turks had strategically sought to eliminate. First the Armenian leaders, then the young men, and now the boys. Only luck had kept Sisak and me alive this long.

"I cannot watch them kill you," my mother said. "Please." That was all she said.

All these years later I still ask myself if I should have left my mother and sister. I ask myself this question almost every day. At the time it was just a fact like so many others we had faced in the last few weeks: Sisak and I were leaving, just as my grandmother was dead by the river, and Armenouhi was dead on a hill of manure. It was a fact no different than the cold wind blowing off the mountains that made us shiver, a thirst there was no water for, thousands of bodies that could not be brought back to life. I know now, as I did then, that Sisak and I had no other choice, but the question returns, or, rather, lives inside me.

We waited, first for darkness, then for the silence that we hoped meant that most of the soldiers were asleep. As the hours passed and the time to leave grew near, my thirst and hunger disappeared, and my heart began to shrink with fear: I, who only a few days before had lived in a house of paintings and tapestries, of English china, crystal decanters, and French cologne, who had never been allowed on the street after dark, who three months before had been punished by my father for putting a mouse in Oskina's bed, was about to cross a hundred or two hundred yards of darkness beneath the searching eyes of how many soldiers?

"Stay low and move as quickly as you can," Sisak whispered. "On your knees and elbows. No matter what happens, keep going."

"Nothing is going to happen," Oskina's voice gently assured me. We were all only voices now, weary sounding in the darkness.

"I'll go first, and you follow," Sisak said. "Knees and elbows—remember."

"Yes," I said, barely audible.

"Don't be afraid, Vahan," my mother said.

Those were to be her last words to me, and that was our last moment together.

It was time. By now I was so frightened that I hardly realized that I was kissing my mother and my sister for the last time—even when I felt my mother's tears on my lips, even when Oskina embraced me and whispered, "Good-bye." It was not really good-bye, it was only good night. I would see them in the morning as I had seen them every other morning of my life.

I turned away from them and began to follow Sisak toward the bank of the river. We crawled over moist earth, then mud, moving as fast and as quietly as we could. Any moment I expected to hear the cry of a soldier or a rifle shot, but there was only the sound of the river and my own beating heart. I looked to the right where the last minutes of sunlight had shown the soldiers to be, but all I saw was darkness.

Sisak was moving faster now, and it was hard for me to keep up. Then faster still, until the bodies near the bank began to block our path. I followed him over the bodies, my arms and legs touching the bare flesh of other arms, other legs. I could feel my stomach rising, and I swallowed again and again to keep it down.

When we reached the river, Sisak was on his feet, and with a suddenness that was almost violent, he took my arm and pulled me into water so cold that it burned, so cold that all the air left my body and my heart clenched like a fist. There was no bottom to the river, and the shock of cold seized my body like a strongman. Every nerve, every muscle contracted, and I began to sink. Instinctively, frantically, I cleared away the cold before me, gulping air into my lungs and trying to keep my face above the poisoned water. I paddled through the path of bodies that my brother had made and reached the opposite bank breathless. Before I knew where I was, Sisak took my arm and pulled me up the bank behind a stand of trees, where we rested and emptied the water from our shoes. We were both shivering, and I could smell the river on my clothes. I looked across the river where my mother and sister remained, but all I saw was the night, and all I felt was the cold.

"Come on," Sisak said, getting to his feet.

Chapter Nine

We walked along the muddy bank, over rocks and fallen branches and patches of snow. The night would have been cold under any circumstances, but our wet clothes made it seem the coldest I had ever known. Like most cold nights, this one came with paralyzing gusts of wind that made me long for the relative warmth of the inn and yesterday's hot sun on the side of my face. I remembered something about a man who lost his nose in the cold, so I cupped my nose and breathed warm air into my cupped hands until my nose thawed and the backs of my hands were frozen. I stopped to rub my arms and legs, but Sisak said we had to keep moving. He did not want to be on the road in daylight. I followed him sullenly, resisting every step I took, wanting only to stop and tear the wet clothes off my body and rub the cold flesh off my bones.

We were now on the road that would lead us back to Bitlis. If we walked all night, Sisak said, without breaking stride, by dawn we would reach Sanis, a village in the eastern part of Bitlis, where there might be Armenians to feed us and give us a place to sleep.

Though this plan seemed only slightly less brutal than the weather, I couldn't help being proud of my brother. If it had been up to me, we would have been walking much slower, shivering and complaining all the way, and here was Sisak, as cold as I, his face and feet and limbs as numb as mine, yet still able to make a plan for us.

I shouldn't have been surprised. Though he wasn't as brilliant as Tavel, or as winning or personable as Diran, whenever a superior measure of courage or leadership or compassion was wanted he produced it like a rabbit from a hat, quietly, as if it were a secret he was sharing with you and hoped you would keep to yourself.

He must have guessed how miserable I was because a mile or so later he stopped and began to rub my arms and legs. "We'll be there soon," he said encouragingly. "Only a few more hours."

I grunted some reply, and he smiled. "This is how steel is made," he said, which was what our father used to say whenever circumstances tested our character, which wasn't very often. "Steel," my father said, "is made strong by fire." And this was our fire. But I did not feel like steel. I felt like cold flesh and bones, and if anything happened to Sisak I did not know what I would do. Without Sisak I would have only myself, and I was not enough, not nearly enough.

"Ready?" he asked.

I wasn't, but I nodded and we started to walk. I knew, of course, that we were much farther than "a few more hours" from Sanis, and being so far from daylight, from food and shelter, made it almost impossible to go on. I wanted to stop. I wanted to tell Sisak that I could not go on. But somehow I kept walking. And when I could no longer walk as myself, I pretended that I was my father, that I had my father's face and my father's will and my father's mind and muscles. I walked as my father would have, with the same expression my father would have worn. I could not keep walking, but my father could; I wanted to stop, but my father didn't. And now I was looking through his eyes at the challenge of the road ahead. My eyes were wet from the cold, and I wiped them with my father's hand. My feet and head and body ached, but I would not stop or even slow down. I was Sarkis Kenderian and I was stronger than the cold, stronger than my thirst and my hunger.

I followed Sisak in this way to the road that led to Sanis, and then toward Sanis itself. Three or four hours later, however, when I saw the scattered lights of the village, my father disappeared and I was myself again, gazing at a dream of lights and wondering how I had come so far.

Trees lined the road that descended to Sanis, and I could see the shapes of houses and the lights in their windows. I was almost delirious now with fatigue and hunger, half walking, half staggering toward the promise of food and water. I knew very clearly that I must keep going. And then I knew very clearly that I couldn't, that I was only a step or two away from falling.

"There," Sisak whispered, pointing beyond the ruins of what might have been a church to the town square a quarter mile away. As we neared the square, Sisak stopped and looked closely at one of the trees. He reached up and picked something from the tree, studied it, then bit it.

"Mulberries," he said.

They were mulberry trees. We had been walking past mulberry trees for the last half mile! Acres of them—all bearing fruit!

I picked and grabbed a handful of the berries and stuffed them in my mouth along with a few leaves. They were cold, and I swallowed the juice as though it were the cool water of the spring I had longed to drink from the day before.

When we could eat no more and our teeth and lips and hands and chins were stained red, Sisak looked at the sky and, seeing no sign of dawn, said, "I think we can rest a minute." These were words as sweet to me as mulberries, and I sank to the ground and leaned against the tree, my head as heavy as a cannonball.

I thought, as I closed my eyes, that I was still Vahan Kenderian, son of Sarkis and Meera Kenderian, safe because I had always been safe. I did not realize that my brother and I had crossed a line, that we had lost more in the last month than the presence of our parents and the protection of our name. I did not realize that Bitlis was no more our home now than Kars or Van, and that the world did not very much care that we had once ridden in coaches and slept in fine beds whose sheets were changed three times a week by a houseman named Karnig. I did not realize that as far as the world was concerned we were nothing more than two vagrants—wet, unarmed, and extremely vulnerable. Therefore, when Sisak said my name and I opened my eyes, the last thing I expected to see was a man standing five feet in front of me with a gun in his hand.

Chapter Ten

"**D**on't be afraid," the man said in Turkish. "I won't hurt you." His beard was black, and his dirt-stained clothes hung from his body as though he were made of sticks. "Are you lost?"

Sisak nodded.

"Stand up."

We stood.

The man looked at me. "How old are you?" he said.

"Twelve," I answered.

The man smiled a friendly smile and took a step toward me. "Pull down your pants."

I unbuttoned my pants and pulled them down to my thighs, assuming that he wanted a new pair of pants to replace the ones he wore.

"Down to your knees," the man said.

I pulled my pants down to my knees, and the man took another step toward me, smiling. "I won't hurt you," he said. Then, with a bony hand so filthy I could not see the skin, he began to rub me. I stood very still, not understanding at first.

"Yes, like that," the man said softly. He was breathing harder now, and then I understood and began to cry.

The man continued to rub me, harder now, his gun at his side, and I thought I could not stand still much longer, that I would have to do something to stop him. But I only cried harder.

Then I heard a thud and the man's arms were around me and we were falling backward to the ground.

Sisak pulled me up, and I saw the rock in his hand, and the blood on the rock. He helped me pull up my pants, took my arm, and we were running as fast as we could to the town square, then past the square to the main street and across to the back streets. I ran as though the memory of the man, his smell and his touch, was chasing me. I stopped and bent forward and tried to throw up, but I couldn't. Sisak took my arm and led me slowly down the street.

"Are you all right?" he said.

I nodded vaguely, still feeling the man's hand touching me.

"Did he hurt you?"

"No," I said, then looked behind me to see if he was there.

"He won't follow us," Sisak said. "I think I broke his head."

I wiped my eyes and started to laugh.

Sisak smiled and put his arm around me. "He'll be the one who has to worry if he finds us," he said.

We walked up and down five or six streets, looking both ways, listening for any sound. The longer we walked, the more certain I became that there was nowhere to go, that even Sisak could not find a place where we would be safe. And I was tired, so tired that I would gladly have gone to prison or even back to the inn if they promised to let me sleep. We walked to the rear of a burned-out stable and slumped against the charred wood boards.

Sisak coughed and closed his eyes. "I have to think," he said.

When I opened my eyes, I knew that the dark blue sky above me was dusk and not dawn, that I had slept many hours, and that I was hungrier than I had ever been in my life. I knew with all the force of a clear mind and a rested body that I would never see my mother and Oskina again.

Sisak was lying on the ground beside me, his arms around his chest as though he were holding a pillow. He looked dead, and when I said his name and he didn't move I began to panic. I said his name again, much louder, and he opened his eyes, to my great relief, coughed, and looked at me.

"What time is it?" he said.

"It's late."

He looked at the sky and nodded. Then he coughed again and sat up against the boards. When it was dark, he tried to stand, and fell back against the stable. I helped him to his feet, assuming that he was weak with hunger or that his legs were as stiff and sore as mine. I did not know he was sick.

We walked to the front of the stable and looked up and down the street. The lamps had not been lit, and all I could see was the dark of buildings against the darker night sky. We crossed the main street, then walked up a narrow side street past locked doors and dark windows. We were looking for luck, for the one friendly stranger, the one open store, but we didn't see any strangers, friendly or otherwise, and all the stores were locked and empty. And the next street was the same, only darker and smelling of something rotten, and the silence of the village was so complete that I was sure our footsteps could be heard a mile in every direction.

"There were houses the way we came," I whispered. "Maybe someone there—"

Sisak shook his head and put his finger to his lips. He had heard something.

I listened.

And then I heard it, too.

We looked around the corner and saw two gendarmes walking in our direction.

"Take off your shoes," Sisak whispered. Without hesitating, I did as I was told while he took off his own. He grabbed my hand, and we ran across the street to the recess of a closed door beneath a stone awning.

Sisak crouched, pulling me down with him. I put my shoes on, my heart pounding as though I had run a hundred miles. The footsteps were louder now, and we listened, as still and breathless as statues.

Sisak tried to open the door behind him, but it was locked. He looked at me, started to say something, and stopped.

The gendarmes had appeared at the bottom of the street.

I could not see their faces or their uniforms, only the red ash of a cigarette that the first one was smoking.

As they walked up our street, Sisak leaned back against the door, and I pressed myself as far into the corner as I could. And now the night that had seemed so dark was not dark enough, and the recess of the doorway where we hid was not deep enough. The gendarmes were almost opposite us now, twenty-five feet away. The first stopped and turned toward our building. The second said something, and the first gendarme held up his hand to quiet him. Now they were both looking at the building. I felt Sisak's hand under me, pushing me up, and I moved my right foot back so that I would be ready to run.

When the first gendarme began to draw his pistol from his holster, Sisak said, "Now," and we broke from the building. I heard a shot, and I was around the corner, running as fast as I could through a maze of streets. I looked behind me, saw that I had not been followed, then ran across the street and crouched behind a butcher shop, looking up and down the street for Sisak. I listened for his footsteps, but I heard nothing, saw no one. I was certain he would find me, certain he was hiding somewhere nearby, in another doorway or just around the corner. We were in the same part of the city, after all, separated by only a few blocks. We couldn't have lost each other.

But we had. And the closer I drew to that realization, the colder the night became and the darker and emptier the street before me seemed. I wanted to look for him, but I was too frightened to move, and every second I waited seemed to bring the gendarmes nearer.

The night before me was an actual presence now, sullen and predatory, and I knew that if I remained here much longer I would either die of fear or the gendarmes would find me. I began to count, hoping that Sisak would appear before I reached fifty. When I reached fifty, I counted to sixty, to seventy. I knew then that he wasn't coming, that I could count to a thousand and he wouldn't come. I heard or thought I heard footsteps behind, turned and saw nothing. I began to count again, trying to keep my legs from walking away with me. When I reached forty, however, I could not remain still any longer. I stood up and began to walk, then to run. At first I thought that I was running home. But my home was six or seven miles away—six or seven miles of soldiers and gendarmes. And then I remembered my friend Pattoo.

Chapter Eleven

Pattoo Altoonian was the best student at St. Matthew's School, a boy any parent would want for a child. He was, by nature, everything I was not—courteous, reserved, bookish, scholastically brilliant, and genuinely modest. A teacher's delight, his hair was always combed, his clothes spotless, his schoolbooks pristine. I returned from school each day looking as though I had been shoveling coal, and he returned looking as shiny as a new coin. Yet, somehow, we became friends, then best friends. Maybe because, in a world of twelve-year-olds, I was a natural leader and he was a natural follower. I do not mean that he lacked character or self-reliance, only that he was as comfortable following me as I was leading him. And our friendship was cemented by the fact that he was inferior to me in almost every way that counted: If we were fishing, I always caught more fish; if we raced to Aberjanian's General Store, I won by a foot; if we climbed a tree, I was the first to touch the highest bough. His brother Vartan and my brother Tavel were best friends, our fathers were successful and respected men, and our homes were among the few in Bitlis that were furnished in the European style.

His mother, Estelle Altoonian, was a sad-smiling, indulgent woman who smelled of powder and perfume, called me dear, gave me salted carrots, cucumbers, and radishes when I came to visit, and always kissed me on the cheek before I went home. Her eyes were warm, worried, and solicitous, and her voice was as soothing and mature as a mother's voice should be. I thought of her as my second mother, and I thought of her house as my second home.

It was the home I ran to that night.

I stood at the top of the stone walk, gazing at the dark windows and the closed front door. The house, lit now by the moon, looked like a ghost of itself, as much a part of the unknown as the streets I had run from. It occurred to me then that it might not be Pattoo's house anymore, that it might be empty or inhabited by strangers, by Turks. I walked cautiously to the door, started to knock, then stopped myself. I stepped away and looked up at the windows, certain now that Pattoo and his family were dead and that I was standing in front of someone else's house, or no one's house. Quickly, as though I were only seconds away from being seen by a gendarme, I walked around the side to the backyard. I opened the door to the toilet, went inside, closed the door, and sat on the floor. I looked at the night through the wood slats above the door, the same night that had driven me from the streets where Sisak still waited.

It was cold, and I rubbed my arms and legs to get warm. I remembered the cold of the river, and I wished that Sisak and I were crossing it again; I wished we were shivering together on the other side of that river, or sleeping beside each other behind the stable, or walking in wet clothes toward Sanis, or even hiding together from the gendarmes. "Now!" I heard him say, and once again I ran the wrong way, once again I lost him. And now I could not go back, I could not wish or pray or will myself back to those streets to follow him as we ran from the gendarmes. I closed my eyes, but I was not tired enough to sleep or to keep from my mind the realization that I might never see my brother again.

The next thing I knew it was morning and someone was saying my name. I opened my eyes and saw the ghost of Pattoo crouched beside me, looking at me strangely, as though it was I who was the ghost. Before I could speak to him or determine whether or not he actually existed, he disappeared. I called after him, but he was gone, and when I finally got to my feet, I saw

Mrs. Altoonian running toward me, holding up the sides of her dress as she ran. It was a sight more beautiful than any I had ever seen, and I cried then, with relief and gratitude, the tears I had not cried the night before.

Mrs. Altoonian took me to the house. I do not know what I expected to see when she opened the back door and I stepped inside—dirt and cobwebs, I suppose, bare floors leading to dark empty spaces, some reflection of the events that had devastated the rest of Bitlis. Instead I was greeted by the same house I had known all my life—the same walls and windows, the same pictures on the walls, the same smell and the same feeling. We went to the breakfast room, where I sat at the same table I had eaten at a hundred times before and watched Mrs. Altoonian close all the shutters, as though it were dusk instead of dawn. I expected her to ask me what had happened, but, thankfully, she didn't. She kissed me on the cheek and looked at me with sad, searching eyes. "You need to eat," she said, and went into the kitchen.

I gazed dumbly at the four place settings, the tea set in the center of the table, the clock and the brown wood cabinet. Nothing had changed. A hundred years had passed and nothing had changed. There had never been a river or an inn, a single body or a single scream. Armenouhi had never died, and Uncle Mumpreh's pockets were still filled with candy. It did not occur to me to ask myself why Mrs. Altoonian had closed the shutters or why I had not seen Vartan or Mr. Altoonian. I needed so much to believe that everything was the same that I had ignored the fact that it could not be.

Pattoo was sitting beside me silently and somehow protectively. He started to say something, then looked away. Mrs. Altoonian came out of the kitchen and set a red dish of bread and eggs before me. I began to eat, ravenously at first, certain that this was only the first of several helpings. But after only a few bites I began to feel full, and after a few more I was so full and so nauseous that I could eat no more—just the thought of eating sickened me. I asked Mrs. Altoonian for a glass of water, which I drank.

No one said a word. It seemed to me that they were waiting for me to speak, to tell them what had happened, and I could not find the right words, or any words, to tell them. I didn't want to tell them. I looked again at the plate of food. I picked up the fork, and it was very heavy, too heavy to hold. My hands were trembling.

"Can you eat a little more?" Mrs. Altoonian asked me.

I shook my head. I wanted to throw up.

"They killed everyone," I heard myself say. And then I told them who they had killed. And how they had killed them. I told them everything, but there was no relief, no freedom from it. I looked at the cabinet and saw that it was meaningless, that the house and its walls and its rugs and its plates and paintings were meaningless because everyone was dead and I would never see Sisak again.

No one spoke for what seemed like a long time. Mrs. Altoonian shook her head, and Pattoo stared at the table in silence. Mrs. Altoonian asked me if I had had enough to eat, and when I said I had, she took my plate back to the kitchen.

"You need a bath," she said, and if I had not known better I would have thought she was angry with me.

The water pots were heated in the fireplace in the garden and taken to the bathing room, where my bath was made. Twenty minutes later I stepped out of the metal tub, my body raw from the scrubbing I had given myself. I dried my hair and dressed, feeling as though a part of me was still crouched behind the butcher shop, still hiding from the gendarmes.

I looked at myself in the mirror, and the face I saw

was not my own. It was the face of a pauper, with hollow cheeks and sunken eyes and a jaw I had never seen before. The hair was tangled and unkempt, the lips scabbed and swollen, and the flesh under the eyes was gray. If I had been lying in a hospital with my eyes closed, I am sure I would have been pronounced dead. I smiled to test the truth of the reflection, and the wretched face smiled back at me.

Mrs. Altoonian was waiting for me when I opened the door. I noticed then that she looked slightly haggard, slightly faded, as though I had not seen her in five years instead of only thirty minutes.

"Come," she said in a toneless voice that did not sound at all like her real voice. "Come with me."

I followed her upstairs, vaguely aware of how quiet the house was and wondering for the first time where Vartan and Mr. Altoonian were. I assumed that she was taking me to Pattoo's room to rest, but we passed Pattoo's room, then hers. She opened the door to what had once been her mother's room, but instead of the familiar bed and dresser, mirror, tables and chair, the room was cluttered with the discarded objects of at least three generations: a broken chair, an unvarnished wood dresser, a three-legged table, old coffee pots, dented brass coffee cups, a spinning wheel. There were nails in the beige walls where paintings had once hung, and the paintings themselves were stacked haphazardly against the walls. Mrs. Altoonian looked back at me then, as though she might speak, but she did not say a word. She walked directly to a green chair sitting in front of a closed door, pushed it aside, then turned to me.

"You know we aren't safe," she said. "No Armenian is safe in Bitlis. You know that."

"Yes," I said, though I had wanted to believe that we were safe.

"The soldiers who came for your father, they came here, too. They took Vartan and my husband." She stopped, pressed her lips together as if to keep herself from crying. "Pattoo and I are allowed to stay here only because the police commissioner is a friend and has some influence. But the gendarmes come once a month, twice a month, to make sure we aren't hiding anyone. If they found you here, they would kill us all. They would kill Pattoo. They would burn down this house. So you must stay here . . ."

She opened the door, and I was looking inside a dark walk-in closet, empty save for a shelf of books at the rear. "All day," she said.

She asked me if I understood, and I said that I did.

She asked me to promise that I would not open the door for any reason. She told me she was sorry. "If Pattoo came to your mother for help, she would have to protect her son, too," she said. Then she kissed me on the cheek and I went inside the closet and she closed the door.

Chapter Twelve

I sat on the floor in the dark. There were so many things to think about that I did not want to think at all. I closed my eyes and began to count. I had never counted to more than five hundred before, so I counted to five hundred, then to six hundred. At that moment I would gladly have traded my life to become a number, to be four or five or fifty-two, with no sorrows and nothing to fear. I would gladly have traded every breath I would ever take to be the light beneath this door, to be the door itself, or the floor where some other boy sat.

For the first time in my life, I actually hated God. All my life I had felt His hand in all the happiness and good fortune that my family and I had enjoyed, and now I felt betrayed. He could have made me follow Sisak if He'd wanted to, instead of letting me run the wrong way. He could have let me see the rock in the soldier's hand in time to warn my grandmother. He could have made me or Sisak or Oskina turn our heads in time to keep Armenouhi from taking the poison. But He had done nothing.

My grandmother would have told me that it was man, not God, who made the misery in the world and that it was only God's grace that made that misery bearable. She would have reminded me that God was always speaking, but man was not always listening. But I didn't care about that now. All I knew was that I had lost everything, and I swung at the air, imagining it was His face I was hitting, His nose I was bloodying, His heart I was breaking. I told Him who He really was in words as blunt as the fists I used to smash and bloody the perfect planes of His perfect face. And, in my mind, He bore it all, let me hate Him, let me hit Him, let His face become bloody until my anger was spent and I couldn't hate Him anymore.

I tried to sleep, but I could not help thinking about my mother and Oskina. I couldn't help seeing my mother's hands in the sunlight by the spring. I wanted so much to kiss away the paleness and the veins that my mouth formed a kiss; I wanted so much to hold her that my arms closed around me as though I had never left her. I wondered for the hundredth time where Sisak was and where he would sleep tonight and what he would eat. I started to count again. One, two, three . . .

A few hours later I heard footsteps, and then the

door opened and it was Pattoo with a bowl in his hands. "Do you want some madzoon?" he said.

Strangely enough, I did. I was actually hungry again, though I hadn't realized it until then. He sat on the floor in front of me while I ate in silence. There seemed to be nothing to say.

When I finished, I handed him the bowl and thanked him.

He asked me if there was anything else I wanted, and I said no and thanked him again. He nodded, and after a moment, with a look of apology, he closed the closet door and I heard him walk away.

I closed my eyes again, and this time I slept. When I awoke, I looked at the light under the door, watched it fade until it was gone. I listened for some sound of life and heard nothing. I began to count.

My cousin Mesok used to paint portraits in the city of Amasia. He told me once that no one really knew what a chair or a glass or a tree or even a blade of grass looked like because no one could see through more than one pair of eyes, from more than one perspective at a time. "If you think you know an object," he said, "move three steps forward or back, or to the right or to the left, and you will see that you do not know it as well as you think."

I realize now that he was talking about more than objects.

Mrs. Altoonian, Pattoo, and I ate dinner in the dining room. We sat on mats around a low, oblong table upon which Mrs. Altoonian had placed a large earthenware bowl of soup. At dinners past there had been Vartan sitting across from me, Pattoo to my right, Mr. Altoonian at one end of the table, and Mrs. Altoonian at the opposite end. Now there were only the three of us, and I was looking at the empty space across from me and the empty space at the head of the table. The walls of the living room were yellow in the lamplight, and the rooms beyond that light seemed empty, abandoned, as though Vartan and Mr. Altoonian had taken the life or light or heart of the home with them and left only the house.

Mrs. Altoonian bowed her head and asked God for His blessings, and we each broke off a piece of bread and dipped it into the bowl. She spoke optimistically, telling us that things would soon be back to normal, that her friend the police commissioner had assured her that the danger to the Armenians still living in Bitlis would soon pass, that the butcher shop was about to reopen, and the dry goods store would be next. She spoke animatedly, almost unceasingly, as though she were trying to create a bridge of words to see herself safely across her own fears.

She said that she expected her husband to return any day, and when Pattoo looked at her strangely, she said, "We don't know he's dead, do we? Have we seen a body? Has anyone told us he's dead?"

"No," Pattoo said.

"Then don't look at me like I'm crazy. If I'm wrong, let me be wrong, let me be crazy."

"I didn't say anything," he protested.

"You look at me! You don't have to say anything. You know how you look at me. I said maybe, *maybe* your father would return. Is that crazy?"

"No."

"Do you want him to come home?"

"Yes," Pattoo said.

"Then let me be crazy." She turned to me. "I'm sorry, Vahan. You shouldn't have to hear this."

I muttered something, and then the table was silent, and Pattoo looked at his bowl, and suddenly I was sitting with two strangers in a house I no longer knew.

After dinner, Mrs. Altoonian made a bed for me on the floor beside Pattoo's bed. She kissed Pattoo, told him in a private voice that she was sorry, then kissed me and turned out the lamp. I listened to her footsteps on the wood floor, then I heard her bedroom door close. Pattoo was lying on his side, looking at me.

"Did your mother talk to herself after they took your father?" he said. He sounded worried.

"I don't know. I never heard her."

"My mother talks to herself. She sits in her room brushing her hair and talking to herself."

"What does she say?"

"I don't know. I think she talks to Vartan. She started after they shot him."

"Who?"

"Vartan."

"Who shot Vartan?" I said, sitting up.

"The soldiers. They took him to the backyard and shot him."

"Your mother said they took him away."

"They shot him," Pattoo said. "We buried him in the backyard."

I stayed with the Altoonians for one week. After only a few days I began to feel like a guest who was wearing out his welcome. I hadn't seen Mrs. Altoonian brushing her hair or heard her talking to herself, but it was clear that she had changed. I heard the change in her voice, and I felt the change in the darkness every night after she kissed Pattoo and turned out the lamp. Dinners were eaten in silence, and every evening when she opened the door to the closet where I had spent my day, she looked more worried than the day before.

On the evening of the seventh day, as Pattoo was taking his bowl to the kitchen, she looked at me and said, "I think it's time for you to go." She said it so calmly, so matter-of-factly, that for a moment I thought that she wanted me to go upstairs. But I knew better. I looked at Pattoo, who was standing in the hall, his back to the table.

"The gendarmes can come anytime," Mrs. Altoonian explained. "And I can't take that chance."

Pattoo turned to his mother. "Maybe we could—"

"No," she said. "He has to leave tonight." She looked at me. "Forgive me," she said.

Very quickly, too quickly for me to realize what was really happening, she gave me a blanket and a small sack filled with bread and cheese and dried fruit. She told me that she was sorry, and then she kissed me and, a little dazed, I shook Pattoo's hand and stepped into the night.

The front door closed behind me.

Chapter Thirteen

I stared at the night, wondering what to do next. I wish I could tell you that I squared my shoulders, gritted my teeth, and faced that most fearsome moment with a brave heart. I wish I could tell you that I discovered reserves of courage inside myself that I had never suspected, and that I became at last my father's son. But I didn't. In fact, it took me a full minute to walk away from the front door, and as I did so, I considered secretly returning to the toilet in the backyard and hiding there for the rest of my life.

Ahead were the shapes and shadows of a world unlit by street lamps, and a silence so deep I could have heard a door close a mile away. I started down the street, trying to shrug off my fear, trying to find my father inside me, but he wasn't there; no one was there.

I looked at each house I passed, wondering which was empty, which was safe. I was too frightened to even consider the possibility of pushing open a gate, turning a doorknob, or looking through a window, so I walked past one house after another, wishing I had said something, anything, to convince Mrs. Altoonian to let me stay.

I don't know how far I walked or how many houses I passed before I saw one whose gate was open. The windows were dark, and the front door was, incredibly, ajar, as if I had been expected. I walked past the gate to the open door and looked inside. As far as I could tell, the house was deserted, but I said hello two or three times to make sure, and when there was no reply I stepped inside and looked at the dark room before me. I don't know where I found the courage to close the front door, but I did and felt exactly as though I had just lowered the lid of my own coffin.

I could see the half moon through one of the windows, and the indifferent light of that moon gradually revealed an empty house with bare walls. In the middle of the room was a toneer, but there was no fire there, or wood or dried dung to make a fire. There were earthenware jugs in a corner of the room, but they were empty. There was straw matting on the floor, but the rugs were gone. The ropes where melons had once hung dangled from the ceiling. There were no stairs, no other rooms, and no key to lock the front door.

I made my way over a creaking wood floor to the kitchen. The window that faced the yard was open, so

I closed it, crept back to a corner of the living room where I could not be seen through the window, and ate a few pieces of dried fruit. I was tempted to cry then, but I could almost hear my father say "Be a man," so I glared at the darkness as a man might and tried to be brave. As it turned out, bravery was out of the question. Not crying was the best I could do. I wrapped myself in my blanket and lay in the dark with my eyes open and felt my aloneness as though it were another body inside me with arms and legs and shoulders. I turned onto my side, but the loneliness turned with me. I prayed for Oskina and my mother and Sisak and myself. I prayed over and over until all my prayers became the one prayer *"G'aghachem"*—"Please"—which I said until I slept.

The next morning I opened my eyes and looked at my new home—whitewashed walls, tan earthenware jugs, yellow matting, dust on the matting. I ate some cheese, looked in the kitchen for food, found nothing, and went to the backyard, where there was no cow, no chickens, and no eggs. Two apricot trees shaded a well in the rear of the yard, and I walked to one of the trees and stared at the small green fruit that was growing beneath its leaves. I had forgotten that it was spring and that trees could still make fruit. I picked one of the apricots off the tree and examined it. Then I bit into it. It was as sour as I knew it would be, but I chewed it and swallowed it and felt the life of it inside me. I started to toss the apricot away, but changed my mind. I put it in my pocket and went back into the house.

I sat down in the middle of the room, thinking I would remain there all day. That was the smart thing to do. The streets were too dangerous; daylight was too dangerous, and Sisak was miles away by now, in another town, in an empty house of his own.

I would sit here all day. I would eat the food Mrs. Altoonian had given me, look out the window at the sunlit street, and watch the morning become the afternoon and the afternoon become the evening. And tomorrow I would do the same. That was the smart thing to do, the safe thing to do.

The problem was, I did not want to be smart. The problem was, I had spent the last seven days in a closet and I could not stay in this house a moment longer. The problem was, I was more afraid of being alone, of never seeing Sisak again, than I was of all the soldiers and gendarmes in Turkey.

I hid my blanket and my sack of food in one of the closets and looked out the window to make sure that the street was empty.

Chapter Fourteen

I closed the door and stepped into the morning, the first I had seen outside a front door in eight days. I had spent so much time in dark corners that I felt exposed in the sunlight, like a black spider crawling onto a white wall. Opening the gate, I looked up and down the street and started to walk, looking left and right, listening for any sound. I was too nervous to see trees or a blue sky, too nervous to see or smell spring. All I saw was danger, and all I felt was fear.

I tried to look like the boy I had been two or three months before, but inside I knew that I did not belong on these streets and that the first soldier who saw me would either shoot me or take me to jail.

The windows of several of the houses were open, the insides dark, and there was about each house something forlorn and incoherent, a look of dishevelment, as though the whole world had grown old overnight, forgotten who it was and how to take care of itself.

Ahead the stores were beginning to appear, and

strangers who might or might not guess that I was Armenian. I walked as casually as I could and tried to look like one of them, to make my face a mask of complacency. They did not know who I was; they did not know that I had spent the last seven days in a closet or that I was looking for someone I had no hope of finding. As far as they knew, I was just another Turkish youth with a family and a home and a destination. And when the bodies began to appear, the oddly posed refuse that had once been Armenian men and women, I glanced at them as cursorily as a Turkish youth might and stepped over and around them as though they were dung or rotten fruit or broken glass. No matter that some had no heads, some no hands or arms or feet. No matter that they might be my neighbors or teachers or friends. If the others did not see them, neither did I.

At first I thought that the boy lying on the opposite side of the street was one more anonymous body. He was on his side, his knees drawn up to his chest, as still as death. I recognized the faded shirt first, then the back of his head, the color of his hair. I knew as I ran toward him that he was dead, that I was about to see my brother's dead face.

I knelt beside him, took his head in my hands, and turned his face to me. It was Sisak, his eyes glazed and half closed, his skin as dry and white as sand. He did not look like Sisak. He looked like the dead I had seen on the road and the dying I had seen at the inn. Like them, he was neither man or woman, young or old. I stopped breathing then and felt something like a very high wave begin to break inside me. I said his name loudly, insensible to anyone who might have heard, as if the sound of his name spoken aloud would return him to me.

"Sisak!"

He looked at me, and his eyes seemed to open a little wider.

Once again I felt something break inside me, and without knowing or caring who might be watching, I lifted him to his feet, put my arm under his, and half walked, half carried him back to the house where I'd hidden.

I laid him on the floor, cradling his head in my hands as though he were an infant. I covered him with my blanket and tried to compose myself. He was very sick, almost unconscious, and I noticed then how shallowly he was breathing. He was hardly breathing at all. I turned his head toward me. "Sisak?" I said. His head moved slightly, and he coughed. "Sisak . . ."

I felt his forehead, as my mother would have, and it was hotter than any flesh I had ever felt, so hot that I ran as fast as I could to the well, filled one of the jugs with water, then ran back to him, afraid that he might stop breathing in my absence. I knelt beside him, raised his head, and poured a little water into his mouth. He drank slowly, some of the water spilling down his chin and onto his chest because my hands were shaking.

I tried to feed him some bread, but he wouldn't eat. I unbuttoned his shirt, poured water on his chest, and smoothed it over his upper body, the cool water becoming warm, then hot under my fingers. I felt his forehead, hoping it might somehow be cooler, but it wasn't. He was on fire.

And I did not know what to do. I was almost frantic now because I did not know what to do. *I* was supposed to be the one who got sick; *I* was supposed to be the one who Sisak nursed back to health. But somehow we had changed places, and now I was his older brother, his doctor and nurse. I was his last and only hope.

I tried again to feed him a little bread, knowing that bread was not enough. He needed medicine. He needed hot tea, garlic, and lemon juice, hot towels on his chest to make him sweat. He needed my mother or my grandmother.

"Sisak," I said. "Sisak . . ."

He looked at me, though he did not seem to see me.

"I'm sorry I ran the wrong way, Sisak. I'm sorry I didn't stay. I'm sorry. I'm sorry I ran away." I touched his hand. "I'm sorry," I said.

He raised his hand a little off the floor, touched his first two fingers with his thumb. He wanted me to take his hand. I took it and felt his thumb softly stroke the side of my hand. "I ran the wrong way, too," he whispered.

In the evening he closed his eyes and slept. The house grew darker, and I listened to the silence of the world outside and watched him, trying to believe that it was only rest he needed. I would not let myself realize how sick he was, and I would not let myself think he could die. But then I would look at him and see that the part that was strong, that had stood above me and made a path for me to follow, was gone.

I took off my shirt, poured water on it, and laid it across his forehead. I gave him water, wishing it was medicine, wishing it was soup or tea, a bed where he could sleep, a nurse to care for him, a doctor to make him well. I held his hand and tried to will him back to life. But his fever would not break, and he mumbled and coughed and tried to turn in his sleep.

"Be steel," I said softly. "Please, Sisak, be steel."

But he was dying. I admitted that to myself now. I

had come up against the hard shapes of life that could not be recast by the magic of my will, and I sat watching him, defeated. I took the apricot out of my pocket and put it in his. Then I said a prayer.

In the morning he shifted under the blanket and licked his lips. I gave him water until he could drink no more.

"How do you feel?"

He made a sound.

"Better?"

No. Not better. I felt his forehead. Not better at all. I took his hand, and he looked at me, opened his mouth to speak, but made no sound. He was looking into my eyes, and I could not tell what he was thinking or even if he saw me. His breathing was almost imperceptible now. Even with my palm an inch from his nose and mouth, I could not feel if he was breathing in or breathing out.

I watched him for several hours, unable to help him, to give him my own breath. I knew what I was waiting for, and I sat frozen as if the realization was a kind of literal cold that precluded any other thought or sensation.

It came very quietly, so quietly that I didn't hear it, I didn't see it. I thought I had been watching him, but it came and I didn't see it. It was not so different from sleep, but I knew before I said his name, before I said it again and touched his shoulder and shook him and lifted his head and kissed him and felt the flesh cooler on my lips.

I started to stand, but something stopped me. I tried again to stand, and again I could not move. Mechanically, I pulled the blanket over his face and stared at it. I lifted the blanket and touched his face and kissed it.

I looked at him for a long time, trying to fill myself with him. I stared at him until he became nothing, the way a word will become nothing if you say it over and over. I stayed with him until the futility of staying became so strong that I stood up.

As if in a trance, I picked up my wet shirt, put it on, and walked out of the house.

Chapter Fifteen

I did not know where I was walking and I didn't care. I didn't care if I was caught and taken to prison, or run through with a sword.

I passed several people on the street, some of whom might have been soldiers or gendarmes, but I didn't look; I didn't have to. I was as free as a ghost or a dying man. What did I have to fear? By the time I heard the shots, I would be dead; by the time I felt the sword, I would be with my family again. Vaguely I knew that I was walking to the spot where Sisak and I had been separated eight days before. I imagined that he was still waiting for me, behind one building or another, and I would tell him about the empty house and the boy I had found on the street. "I thought it was you," I would say.

"I've been here for eight days," Sisak would reply. "What took you so long?" Then he would take me to the house where he lived, and it would be twice as big as mine, with food in all the cupboards, and a bed where I could sleep, and a key to lock the front door.

"Get some rest," he would say, "I'll be right here."

But even as I lay down on that imaginary bed, I knew that he was two or three miles behind me, on the floor where I had left him. And I knew that when I reached Sanis I would keep walking because there would be no reason to stop.

Something clutched my arm, spun me around.

"Where are you going?"

I looked at the gendarme but said nothing. I did not have to say a word to anyone anymore.

He asked me my name, but I did not answer.

"You're Armenian?"

I shrugged.

The gendarme tightened his grip and pulled me down the street. I did not know where I was being taken and I didn't care. It would be a place to die or a place to sleep, so I was glad to go along.

He was walking so fast that I had to run to keep up, and his grip was so tight that my wrist began to ache. We passed the road to the prison and turned onto the street that led to my old school, St. Matthew's. I recognized the trees that lined the street, and then the squat, suddenly ominous façade of the school itself. For a moment I doubted my own eyes. Why was

I being taken to school instead of to prison or the inn or the hangman? It made no sense, but, on the other hand, it was no longer my concern.

I was dragged up three tiers of stone steps to the double doors of the entrance, where a soldier stood. The soldier opened the door, and the gendarme pulled me inside.

The long hall was empty, and all the classroom doors were closed. Through darkened windows I saw rows of desks and closed shutters. We continued past the court-yard, its fountain now dry, down the tree-shaded brick path that led to the closed doors of the auditorium, guarded now by two soldiers. One of them opened a door, and I was pushed inside. The door closed.

I saw the darkened aisles first, then the familiar stage, the rows of benches. Here and there, children appeared—on the benches, on the stage, sitting and slumped against the walls. There must have been sixty or seventy of them. Most were near death. Some were already dead. Among the faces, I recognized some of my schoolmates—boys I had passed in the hall, boys who had sat three rows behind me, who had eaten their lunches at other tables.

Perhaps for a moment I was shocked or sickened by their condition. And then it was just another sight, the fiftieth or the five hundredth blow, soundless now, and painless, and no more surprising than a headless corpse or a starving infant.

I lay down on one of the benches and closed my eyes. I remember thinking that if so many could die, then I could die, too, that it must be easy to die. All I had to do was relax, pull back the bolt of the flesh, and release my soul.

I asked God to please let me die, to please take my soul into His kingdom. I was certain then that I would begin my long ascent to heaven, to Sisak and Armenouhi and the arms of my mother and father, but I didn't. I expected to feel God's fingers loosening my soul from my body, but I felt no such thing.

I lay on that bench numbly, for minutes or hours, unable to sleep, unwilling to sit up or to stand. For one absurd instant I actually believed that I was hovering halfway between the bench and the domed ceiling above me, but when I opened my eyes I was still on the bench, no closer to heaven than the guards outside the door. I began to worry then because I realized that there weren't going to be any shortcuts. I was going to perish slowly and uncomfortably over a period of days, not seconds. I was going to waste away in wordless, breathless misery, in coughing spasms and delirium that could last eight, nine, even ten days. How long had Sisak waited to die? How long had Sisak been lying on the street before I found him? If God Himself had asked me if I was ready to die, I would have said yes. If my mother or father had appeared before me and asked me if I wanted to return with them to heaven, I would have gone along. But to wait eight or nine or ten days? I did not have the patience to wait ten days to die.

I opened my eyes. I knew then, hopelessly, that dying on this bench in this auditorium was out of the question. I had to escape.

But there was no way out. The double doors were locked, and the only windows were twenty-five feet above me. I was sitting in a box, sealed and guarded, with no way out.

Some, when faced with an impossible task, become fiercely alert and attack the problem from every angle. They measure space and calculate time. They build pyramids from stones of logic, and at the very top of the pyramid, at the point where all the corners of the stones meet, they find their answer.

I chose to daydream: I looked around the auditorium, imagining that some secret, undetectable portion of one of the walls was actually a door, or that the floor beneath my feet concealed a subterranean stairway that led to freedom. But there was no magic here, no secret stairways, no trapdoors. It was only a box, sealed and guarded.

In retrospect, it is not surprising that I finally remembered the toilets. What is surprising is that the soldiers forgot about them. There were four wood floors, each with a hole cut in the center. The circumference of each hole was almost two feet, and each descended to the river that ran below the school.

I was on my feet, half walking, half running to the closed door, which I prayed had not been locked. I pushed down on the handle and the door opened. I closed it behind me and walked across the tiled entry to one of the partitioned toilets, studied it for a moment, then looked at another, then another. Not one looked wide enough for a boy half my size.

And now I wondered how far I was going to fall. And into what depth of water? I put my head down one of the holes and listened, expecting to hear the sound of the river, but I heard nothing. The river was dry. I was going to fall twenty, thirty, forty feet to a dry riverbed.

I was beginning to feel light-headed now, almost faint with fear or fatigue or hunger. If I was going to do it, it had to be now.

Slowly, with my hands on either side, I lowered one leg, then the other, down the hole. I could feel the empty space below my feet. To make my body narrower, I raised one arm over my head and pressed the other against my side. My hips and waist cleared easily, but I could feel the hole closing around my shoulders. I twisted left and right, but the more I twisted the tighter the hole became.

And now I was stuck. I could not go down another inch. I squirmed and twisted—but the hole was too small. I rested a moment, then, with all the strength I possessed, I tried to screw my body down that hole, twisting left, then right, left and right with everything I had, with all my rage and all my despair, with Armenouhi clutching her stomach and Sisak dead on the floor, I tried to twist myself, will myself down, down an inch, half an inch, a quarter of an inch. And it was no good. I could not go through. And now the room seemed darker, and there was no air left to breathe. I had breathed it all and my strength was gone. I tried once again, twisting and squirming, but it was hopeless. I only needed an inch or two more, but my strength was gone.

I closed my eyes and my body went limp. I opened my eyes and the room was black. And then I was falling inside myself, into black.

I awoke inhaling water instead of air. I did not know if the water was a river or an ocean or a lake. Ahead was sunlight, and I swam for it, then across to a green bank.

———

I scrabbled a few feet up the bank, where I collapsed, not knowing where I was or how I had gotten there. I remembered then that Sisak was dead, that this was the day he died. He was still alone in that empty house.

I struggled up the bank to the road that led back to town and walked numbly for what seemed like hours. I was walking home from school, following the same path I had followed all my life, yet I seemed to be someone else entirely.

I could see Aberjanian's General Store ahead. The store was empty, and the door was locked. Through one of the broken windows I saw the counter where the jars of candy had been. Only the scales were left now.

There were three or four stores farther ahead, but their doors were closed and I was too tired and too cold to look through the same grimy windows at the same bare walls, counters, and shelves. I walked to the rear of the general store and sat against the wall. I was shivering. I took off my pants and squeezed out the water. I took off my shirt, saw it laying across Sisak's forehead, and began to cry.

Chapter Sixteen

I awoke the next morning to the faraway sound of children's voices, the sound of school halls and playing fields, a sound I could not be hearing on an abandoned street in Bitlis. I listened, my mind still blanketed by sleep, certain I was still dreaming. Yet, when I opened my eyes, the voices remained.

I got quickly to my feet and walked to the main street, where I saw fourteen or fifteen children begging in front of the stores I had given up for empty the day before. Because the only victims I had seen in the last two months had been Armenian, I assumed that these were Armenians, too. As I got closer, however, and heard the language they were speaking, I realized they were Turkish. Probably refugees, driven from whatever towns and cities the war had reached. They were dressed in worn, ripped, or tattered clothing, and their unwashed arms and legs were almost as thin as Sisak's had been. They moved as one, spoke as one, running from one person to another, from those who would not give to those who might. "I'm hungry," they said. "I need food. Please, Lady. Please, Mister." A few handed them a piece of bread or a portion of cheese. Some handed them coins; others turned away.

I, too, was hungry, but I had never begged. And the idea of begging shamed and disgusted me. Beggars were unshaven men with greasy hair and glassy stares and clothes that had never been clean. I had seen them on my way home from school, depressed and cautionary figures. If one spoke to me, I did not answer. If one asked me for money, I tossed it to him because I knew that he was poisonous and that the disease of failure or bad luck or alcoholism was contagious and could be transmitted by touch.

I was not a beggar, but I knew as I watched the children that I *would* beg, that I *had* to beg. It was not a decision that I questioned or doubted, but a fact as real and as stark as my empty stomach. Who would give me food if I did not beg for it?

At that moment, a woman carrying a cloth sack stepped out of the bakery. Without allowing myself a second to reflect on what I was about to do, I started toward her, bowing my head a little so that she could not see my face, so that she would not know that the beggar approaching her was Vahan Kenderian, son of

Sarkis and Meera Kenderian. "I need food," I said in Turkish. "Could you please—"

Before I could finish my sentence, my hand was one of seven other hands, and my voice could not be heard above the pleading of eight or nine other voices. I shouldered and shoved the children aside, my eyes never leaving the woman's hand, which was now the center and sole support of my existence. I watched it disappear into the cloth bag, and when it reappeared a moment later holding a piece of bread, I snatched the bread from her fingers and ran down the street as fast as I could, stuffing it into my mouth and looking back to make sure I wasn't being followed.

It was the most triumphant and humiliating moment of my life.

I was not always so successful. Other hands were sometimes faster than mine, other voices louder, other bodies stronger, but I managed to come away with enough bread and cheese to keep my stomach from aching. By the end of the day, having chased rolling coins and licked the smallest crumbs off the palms of my hands, I was a beggar, too tired to wonder or to care whether or not I should be ashamed.

That night I sat against the back wall of the general

store as though I had been sitting there all my life. I ate the food I had saved, vaguely conscious of the darkening sky and the long minutes of dusk settling upon the empty streets. I closed my eyes and saw nothing, felt nothing. My heart was closed and locked.

For several weeks I jostled and pleaded for food, ran from those who would not give to those who might. At night I covered myself with newspapers and shivered behind Aberjanian's General Store. I awoke shivering in the middle of the night and rubbed my arms and legs for hours to keep warm.

I discovered I had a temper, and that hunger seemed to shorten its fuse. If anyone, boy or girl, tried to push me aside, I pushed harder. If anyone wanted to fight, I was ready. I moved and thought and spoke only for food. There was nothing else. There had never been a home, or a mother and father; there had never been servants, blankets, or a bed of my own. And each day, I felt less and less like myself and more and more like a beggar. And as time passed, it did not seem to matter what a beggar did, or whether or not a beggar said "please" or "thank you" or who he pushed aside or where he slept or what he ate. All that mattered was whether or not the beggar survived. And I was surviving.

As I grew thinner and my clothes became the color of the dirt streets, I began to hate every Turk I begged from. Even when they smiled, even when they were generous. I hated their faces, the clothes they wore, the money in their pockets, their language and their blood. I hated them for having food to eat and homes to return to. I cried because I hated them—tears of rage and self-pity, tears to annihilate the world, and beg it for a second chance. I cried because my skin itched under my clothes and because my clothes were filthy and because I smelled like the street I had been begging on. I cried because all my tears could not make a blanket for me to sleep under or clean clothes to wear.

One cold night, a few hours before dawn, I stood up and paced back and forth to warm myself. I walked around the store to the windy street and saw, below the steps of the bakery, four Turkish children huddled under two blankets. I walked past them and on up the street, past the dark forms of other sleeping children, and farther still. I thought I was going to another part of the city, to find another empty house. And then I knew that I was going back to the Altoonians'.

Chapter Seventeen

I went to the Altoonians' backyard, opened the door to the toilet, sat on the floor, and waited.

When I finally saw the light of morning, I walked to the back door and knocked. I tucked in my shirt and put my hands in my pockets so that Mrs. Altoonian would not see how dirty they were. I patted the dust off my pants, picked off some of the crusted dirt with my thumbnail, and tried to look as presentable as possible. I did not need a mirror to know it was hopeless.

If I had had an ounce of my father's pride or character, I never would have returned. She had already told me to go away; she had already told me that I was a danger to her family. And still I had come back. What would I say when she opened the door? What could I say? I would ask her for food and water and a place to sleep—just for a day or two. If she said no and told me to go away, I would go. I wouldn't beg anymore.

I knocked again, harder this time, knowing I would

beg, knowing I would do anything to convince her to let me stay.

I heard footsteps; then I heard the bolt of the door retract.

The door opened and I was facing Mrs. Altoonian. Without a word, she kissed me and took me inside.

I now knew enough about the world to know that I did not ever want to set foot outside the Altoonians' front door again. I knew enough about the night, about the cold, about hunger and humiliation to know that there was no such thing as pride. The fear that Mrs. Altoonian would soon tell me that I had to leave haunted me every minute of every day. It was in Pattoo's room after she turned out the light; it was in my dreams, and it stared back at me when I awoke in the middle of the night. Hoping to enter into her good graces, I tried to be as helpful as I could. Every morning I folded my sheets, put them in the dresser, and returned the mattress to Vartan's room. I did not allow myself to eat too much, and I always helped her clear the table and wash the bowls and dishes. "You don't have to do that, Vahan," she would say, but I was happy to do it. Perhaps if I did enough things, she would not want me to leave.

After dinner, on the evening of the seventh day, I sat paralyzed in my chair, waiting. It had been seven days the first time, so I had spent most of the day thinking about what I could say or do to convince her to let me stay a little longer. But the evening passed and she did not say a word. I survived the eighth evening, as well. And the ninth and tenth. And then I began to think that maybe she did not want me to leave, that maybe I would never have to leave.

I was wrong: On the evening of the eleventh day, she told me that she had gone to see Selim Bey, the ex-governor of Van. She told me that he was living in my family's house. She told me that he and my father had worked together in Van, where my father had practiced law in an Armenian court. She told me that the governor had great respect for my father and that he was a fair and honorable man.

And I did not believe my ears. Two months before, the name Selim Bey had been on the lips of every Armenian who had escaped from Van. "The butcher of Armenians" they called him. He was also known as the "Horseshoer of Bashkale" for his practice of nailing horseshoes to the feet of his victims. How many hundreds, how many thousands of Armenian men had he marched out of the city and murdered? How many homes had he burned to the ground? By his orders, mothers and infants were killed and the heads of his more influential victims were sometimes mounted on poles outside the government building.

And this monster, this madman, was living in my home, the home of my family. And Mrs. Altoonian had visited him, had spoken with him. And called him a fair and honorable man. Why, I did not know. I could not guess.

I found out three days later, when she called me into the living room and told me that all our problems were solved. The governor, she said, had agreed to let me stay with him. "You're going back to your own home," she said exultantly.

It was supposed to be good news. It was supposed to be the best news I had ever heard. So I made my face as happy as hers, and thanked her, and asked her when I was leaving.

"Tomorrow," she said.

The next morning I ate my breakfast in silence, as though it were my last meal, knowing that I was on my way to the house of a murderer and that whatever could have happened to me on the street or at the inn could happen to me there. I kept hoping that Mrs. Altoonian would change her mind, that at the last moment she would realize that she loved me and could not let me go. But either she did not have that realization, or she had it and ignored it.

After breakfast she filled a bag with fruit and bread and cheese and pressed the bag into my hand. "I know you're going to be happy," she said.

I nodded manfully, but when I heard the knock on the door, my heart jumped.

"Go upstairs, Pattoo," Mrs. Altoonian said.

Pattoo and I faced each other, and in the air between us were all the races we had run, all our adventures, and the awareness that we would never see each other again. There was so much to say that we said nothing. He patted me on the shoulder and smiled awkwardly. Then he walked out of the kitchen.

I followed Mrs. Altoonian to the front door, to the end of the world. I stood a few feet behind her, warily, certain that on the other side of that door were two soldiers who had come to kill the second-to-last living Armenian male in Bitlis. She opened the door, and I saw a small, officious-looking man wearing a brown suit and spectacles. The man nodded once in greeting. "I am Selim Bey's assistant," he said to Mrs. Altoonian. "Is this the boy?"

"This is Vahan Kenderian," Mrs. Altoonian said.

I took a step forward, but the man did not smile or shake my hand. "Come with me," he said.

I embraced Mrs. Altoonian, and for an instant she was my mother and I was saying good-bye once again. She kissed me on the forehead, and, certain it was all a terrible mistake, I followed the man out the door.

On the street I saw my family's carriage with one of the governor's horses in harness. The man stepped inside the carriage as if he owned it and sat where my father had always sat. I sat across from him. Beside me was the empty seat where my mother should have been.

As the carriage jerked forward and rolled away, I folded my arms across my chest and felt my heart beating against the palm of my right hand. I uncrossed my arms and glanced out the window, then at the man sitting across from me. Although he was not a soldier and carried no rifle, I did not trust him, nor did I trust that I was really being taken to my home. Any second I expected the carriage to turn onto the road that led to the school or the prison or Goryan's Inn.

But when we actually turned onto the lane that led to my home, I felt no relief at all. I had walked to school on this lane, run races against Oskina, climbed trees, picked fruit, and ridden horses. Now the lane was deserted, and all I saw was myself and my family being led out of the city by the soldiers.

Outside my window, the long white garden wall came into view. I gazed at the wall, remembering Tavel and Diran, and hearing the shots that had killed them as clearly as I had heard them that day. Beyond the wall, I saw my home, but it did not look like my home anymore. It looked like any other house, only larger and more imposing.

The carriage turned onto the road that ran alongside the house, and turned again onto the road that led to the stable. Two men swung open the gate, and the carriage slowly rolled inside. I was home. But, of course, it wasn't really home anymore. It was just another dead body, another deserted street.

I stepped down from the carriage, expecting to be taken to my room, where I would change into my own clothes and wait until the governor wished to see me. But before I had taken three steps, Selim Bey's assistant took my arm and led me into the stable, a dark place of creaking wood planks, narrow, dusty streams of sunlight, and white stalls that Sisak and I had painted three summers before.

"Your job," he said, "is to keep this stable clean and dry. The governor does not want any mess on the ground. When the horses do their business, you put it in the pail. You may empty the pail in that trough. Do you understand?"

"Yes," I said.

"You will stay in this stable all day and all night.

Whatever you need will be brought to you. You will not go inside the house for any reason. You will not bother the governor. Food and water will be brought to you twice a day. Your clothes will be washed once a week. I will thank the governor for you."

BOOK TWO

Chapter Eighteen

After three weeks, I still hadn't seen Selim Bey. Every day, I waited for the stable door to open and the doorway to be filled by his terrible presence. I wondered what I would say to him, how I would behave. I was determined to be a fearless representative of my family and my people. I would look him in the eye and answer whatever questions he put to me firmly and succinctly. If he asked me my name, I would simply say "Vahan" or perhaps "Vahan, sir," as I did not want to be unnecessarily disrespectful and lose my life. If he asked me how old I was, I would say "Twelve." If he asked me if I had enough to eat, I would say "Yes" or "Yes, sir." If he asked me if I liked living in a stable, I would say "No" or "No, sir." If he asked me why, I would say "Because my mother and father did not raise me to live in a stable, sir." If he considered my remarks discourteous and decided to kill me with his bare hands, or deprive me of food and water, so be it. I would not grovel for a butcher. Nor would I smile or shake his hand or ingratiate myself in any way. I would be my father's son: proud, aloof, and unbending.

Every morning, I groomed the horses and cleaned the dung from their stalls, certain that this was the day I would meet the madman. But he never came. To occupy myself, I made a target on the wall with the dung and threw rocks at it. I quietly sang Armenian songs, and talked to the horses, and slept, and waited for my meals.

For breakfast I was given bread and yogurt. For dinner I was given bread, and either bulgur and onions or stew. The soldier who brought my meals always dropped the tray a foot from the ground so that some of the food fell in the dirt. He laid the jug of water on its side so that half the water spilled out. And I did not say a word. I was afraid to even look at him.

He called me a coward, he called my people animals and traitors. And I said nothing. I stared at the ground and waited for him to go away. And after he was gone, I killed him a thousand times in a thousand different ways. I took his rifle and killed him with his bayonet; I cut his throat with his own knife; I shot him in the face, in the heart, again and again.

At night I lay on my bed of straw under the blanket I had been given. There were four lamps on the walls, but I rarely used them. I felt safer in the dark.

Sometimes, I tried to imagine what the governor looked like. I saw him as a fat man with a blubbery gray face, oily skin, and dead black eyes. Sometimes I saw him as a huge, muscular man of limitless power and cruelty. But whether he was fat like a sultan or muscular like a strongman, he was always shrewd, always smiling, always speaking fair and honorable words with a teacup or a wine glass in his hand.

As the weeks passed, he loomed larger and larger in my imagination until finally he became the most vivid and pervasive presence in my life. I could almost see him lying on my father's bed, reading by the light of my father's lamp. In my mind he had become as broad as a shadow on the wall, with eyes as hypnotic as a candle flame. I had to remind myself that he was only a man, only flesh and blood, only a thug who did not have the good manners to present himself to his prisoner, and I renewed my vow to stand up to him when we finally met.

Unfortunately, it is one thing to stand up to a phantom, and another to stand up to a human being: One morning the stable door opened and I saw a man standing in the doorway, his head and upper body rimmed in sunlight. At that distance he could have been the soldier who brought my food, the assistant who had transported me to the stable, or any one of a thousand other soldiers or assistants. But somehow I knew who it really was, and in an instant I was on my feet, not as the defiant representative of my people but as a twelve-year-old boy whose mouth was suddenly dry and whose legs had suddenly turned to jelly. When he closed the door and the sunlight disappeared, I was looking at a well-dressed man (English suit, perfectly creased trousers, silk tie) with a short black-and-gray beard.

"You are Vahan Kenderian?" he said. It was a pleasant voice, calm and authoritative.

"Yes," I replied, as though he had asked me if I was ready to die.

The man advanced toward me, and I felt myself begin to shrink inside. Instinctively, I put my hands in my pockets.

"I am Selim Bey," the man said. "I knew your father."

I said nothing, only looked at him, at the clear black eyes and the black pouches of flesh beneath the eyes. Something about his presence or his posture made everything in the stable seem smaller.

"I'm sorry it's taken us so long to meet," he said. "I've been very busy. You are comfortable here? You have enough to eat?"

"Yes," I said. Then, despite myself, "Thank you."

Selim Bey looked at me with eyes that seemed to see through me. "Why are you afraid?" he said.

I did not answer. He was three feet from me, and he was the Horseshoer of Bashkale, and I could not utter a single word. I noticed the perfectly manicured fingernails and, on the third finger of his right hand, the biggest gold ring I had ever seen.

"You are here because you are Sarkis Kenderian's son. You were not brought here to be harmed."

I nodded meekly, and tried to meet his eyes.

"I was sorry to hear he was called. If there was any way I could have stopped it, I would have. But these things . . ." He shook his head. "Enver Pasha himself couldn't have stopped it." He glanced at my blanket and mattress of straw. "Is it cold for you at night?"

I nodded, surprised by his concern.

"But you have enough to eat?"

"Yes."

"Good. It is very hard for Armenians to find food these days. But I'll make you a promise: As long as I eat well, you will eat well."

An empty space was offered for me to thank him, and I did. And now I knew why Mrs. Altoonian had trusted him, and why she had said he was a fair and honorable man. If I hadn't known who he was, I would have trusted him, too.

He looked at the target of dung on the wall, and a trace of a smile appeared on his lips. He looked again at my blanket, then walked to the stalls where the horses were kept. Watching him made it easy to forget that he was a butcher of Armenians and not simply a debonair and prosperous businessman.

He took something out of his pocket, fed it to one of the horses, and walked back to me.

"Thank you for grooming my horses," he said. "Not many boys do more than is asked of them." Again, the smile appeared, and this time I almost found myself smiling, too.

"I'm glad we met," he said, extending his hand.

Without thinking, without hesitating, I shook that soft dry hand, and did not realize what I had done until after he left the stable.

That evening I was given twice my usual ration of food, and this time the soldier did not spill the water or drop the tray on the ground or utter a single word against me. He entered the stable silently, placed the tray before me, and disappeared.

That night, as I lay under my blanket, I thought about the unusual man I'd met that morning: his courtesy, his praise, his hand shaking mine. He had treated me not like an Armenian orphan, but like the son of a man whose wealth and influence he admired. I tried to remember that he was a murderer, that he was responsible for making widows of women like my mother and orphans of boys like myself. But as hard as I tried, I could not imagine him ordering anyone's death or burning anyone's house to the ground. "If you want to know a man," my grandmother once told me, "look at his eyes and his mouth." I tried to remember Selim Bey's eyes, tried to remember if I had seen anything monstrous or despicable there. But they were only eyes, clear and penetrating. Perhaps my grandmother would have seen a murderer there, but I did not.

As the weeks passed, I was given a pillow, an extra blanket, new clothes, and new shoes. The governor even allowed me to ride his horse outside the stable. At first I wanted no part of his generosity. I wanted only to be left alone, to eat and sleep and survive until it was safe for me to return to the Altoonians'. I was still an Armenian, after all, and he was still the enemy.

But as weeks turned to months, it became harder and harder to ignore his friendship, harder and harder to imagine a monster in this well-dressed, well-spoken, distinguished-looking man. I did not want to be Mrs. Altoonian, telling myself that he was fair and honorable, yet I had seen no evidence that he wasn't. He had never raised his voice to me, never threatened me or struck me. How could I hate such a man? And how could I be sure he was a monster? I hadn't seen him kill anyone or burn down anyone's house. I hadn't seen him mount anyone's head on a pole or nail horseshoes to anyone's feet. I did not doubt that those events had taken place, but how could anyone be sure that Selim Bey was to blame? He wasn't like the soldiers who had killed Diran and Tavel. He was not like the gendarme who had dragged me to the auditorium. He had offered me his protection. He had even offered me his advice:

"In this world," he told me, "there is no such thing as a country or a flag or a right or wrong cause. There is only yourself. You are your own flag, your own cause and country. In the end, if you are poor and cold and hungry, no one will care if you were a patriot or an honest man. All they will see is a beggar, an unsuccessful animal. Do you understand?"

He always asked me, rather imperiously, if I understood.

I did. But did I agree? After a time, yes. His philosophy seemed, then, only an adult refinement of my own youthful objectification of human beings, of the odd, luckless figures I had observed as a rich man's son. And, too, I was wearing the clothes *he* had given me. I was warm at night because he had given me a second blanket. My belly was full because he gave me all the food I could eat. I was not lonely because he visited me in the stable two or three times a week. I *wanted* to see his point of view, I wanted to see the world through the eyes of my protector. Only later did I learn that while he was allowing me to ride his horse and giving me extra blankets and new clothes, he was also (with the help of two or three hundred Turkish troops) killing off the last of the Armenians in Bitlis and confiscating their valuables. Only later did I realize how inhuman a well-dressed, well-spoken, charming man could be.

Chapter Nineteen

Early in the spring, the governor told me that we were going to Kars.

The following day, as I rode his horse past the front of the house, I saw several soldiers loading wagons with my family's belongings. I recognized my mother's dresser, the desk from my father's study, the lamp my grandmother had read by. They were lying in the middle of the street, about to be loaded by rough hands onto the flat beds of three anonymous wagons, and I felt suddenly as though my heart were being torn in two, for I could not reconcile the boy who was sitting on Selim Bey's horse with the boy whose life lay on the street before him. In self-defense, I suppose, I turned the horse sharply and kicked it hard, until we were running full speed back to the stable.

I left for Kars two days later—not with the governor, as I had hoped, but with a lean, sour-looking soldier with hollow cheeks, a wiry black beard, and hands as furry as the paws of a bear.

When I stepped onto the wagon, the soldier did not look at me or acknowledge my presence. His jaw, however, tightened perceptibly, and just before he shook the reins, he touched his rifle—menacingly, I thought.

Being a thirteen-year-old, undersized, unarmed Armenian boy who could be shot, stabbed, beaten, or abandoned by the man sitting next to me, I felt that it was in my best interest to act as friendly as possible.

So I asked him his name.

The soldier did not answer, so I repeated the question, a little louder. The soldier looked at me in a way that assured me that if I said one more word, asked one more question, made one more sound, he would shoot me, strangle me, or throw me off the wagon.

"Shut up," the look said.

And I did. In fact, for the first hour or so I sat as stiff as a board, afraid even to clear my throat.

In silence we passed Goryan's Inn. It was just as I had left it the year before, only now the front door was boarded, the hill of manure gone. I looked up at the boarded window, our window. I looked at the morning my family and I stood in the raw sunlight, waiting for the march. I could almost see the soldiers on horseback, almost hear the cries for food and water.

We continued toward Kars along a placid country

road identical to the one my family and I had walked as prisoners. Trees as pleasant and leafy as any I had ever seen lined either side of the road, and wildflowers grew profusely in the grassy fields beyond them. Farther on, I saw the bones of other Armenian prisoners from other marches. I saw the tattered, dusty rags that had once been shirts and shawls and pants and dresses. I saw myself and my family staggering forward, our faces dusty and our mouths dry. I could still feel the thirst and hunger I had felt then; I could still hear the voice behind me say, "Why don't they kill us now?"

As we drove on, I began to look for the footprints of the hundreds or thousands who had been forced to walk this road, but, of course, they had blown away, and a few miles later there was no smell, no sight left to act as witness to what had happened here.

When we reached Kars, I saw that most of the population was gone, and that many buildings had been destroyed. I saw the rubble of mud and stone where Armenian churches had been, dry earth and weeds where Armenian gardens had been, empty frames where the doors and windows of Armenian businesses had been.

And it was not the war. Or rather, it was the other

war, the one no one had declared, the one the snow could bury and the wind could blow away.

The wagon climbed a steep road that led to a huge building that looked like a palace. The double doors were painted bright red, and all the windows had maroon awnings like a fine European hotel. Thinking that this might be my new home, I broke my three-day silence to ask the soldier if this splendid edifice was a house. Without looking at me, the soldier uttered his first and last word of our journey.

"Consulate," he said.

Twenty minutes later, I was taken to the stable behind the consulate and given my blankets and my pillow and a day's ration of food. I sat against one of the walls and gazed at the stalls of horses. I had traveled eight days on a hard board over bumpy roads with as grim a companion as I could have imagined, only to find myself back where I had started.

I should have been so lucky.

Chapter Twenty

The problem with loneliness is that, unlike other forms of human suffering, it teaches us nothing, leads us nowhere, and generally devalues us in our own eyes and the eyes of others. It lies upon the soul lightly or heavily, depending on one's age and one's luck, and swiftly transforms the heartiest of souls into a living ash of spiritual doubt and despair. It is impervious to medicine, common sense, wisdom, humor, hope, or pride. It simply comes, sits in the center of the heart where it cannot be overlooked, and abides.

I did not know what loneliness was until I came to Kars.

Except for the soldier who brought my food to the stable, I saw no one. Each day arrived with a sixteen- or seventeen-hour burden of time, and when the day was over and all the empty hours had been spent, there was nothing to do but sleep and wake up and begin again.

Every day, I expected Selim Bey to visit me, but he

never did. I wondered where he was and why he was avoiding me. Hadn't he said *we* were going to Kars? Maybe he was in the consulate and didn't want to see me. Maybe I had disappointed him in some way and he never wanted to see me again. I asked the soldier who brought my meals if Selim Bey was in the consulate, but the soldier did not reply, or even look at me.

To pass the time, I made a new target on the wall, groomed the horses every morning, and daydreamed about killing myself. Several times a day, I put an imaginary gun to my temple and pulled an imaginary trigger. Sometimes I withdrew a pirate's dagger from its sheath and, both hands clutching the hilt, drove it into my chest, twisting it as deep into the loneliness as I could. I spent one long day making a killing noose out of a piece of rope, then putting the noose around my neck and pulling the free end as hard as I could until I realized that all I was giving myself was a rope burn.

At night I lay under my blankets and counted to calm myself. I felt my loneliness on my skin, in my chest and stomach. I wanted to cry in my mother's arms. I wanted to beat down the walls of the stable with my fists, and swim in rivers, and talk to my own people in my own language. And when I thought I could not stand another day, the stable door opened late one afternoon, and a soldier I had never seen before entered with a young girl. "She's going to stay with you," he said, and closed the door.

It seemed at first too good to be true, and I was as dumbfounded by this great luck as I had once been by misfortune.

The girl had black hair and wore a sweater over her dress. Her feet were swathed in strips of cloth, and her ankles were streaked with dirt and dried blood. I could not see her face because her head was bowed, but she did not look much older than nine or ten.

I approached her doubtfully, as one would approach a mirage, afraid that if I moved too fast or too abruptly, if I reached out my hand or spoke too soon, she would disappear.

"My name is Vahan," I said, the first Armenian words I had spoken to anyone but myself in over a year.

The girl raised her head a little, and I saw the large black eyes, the small red mouth, and the green and black bruise that covered the entire left side of her face.

"My name is Seranoush."

She looked dazed, the way my mother had looked after Diran and Tavel were shot. There were shadows under her eyes, and her lips were wrinkled like the lips of an old woman. Seeing her condition I wanted to reassure her and comfort her and be her friend. All at once. But I did not know how to begin.

"I come from Bitlis," I said.

Seranoush nodded, avoiding my eyes. "I come from Moosh," she said, softly, to the floor. "Are they going to kill us?"

It was a stunning question coming from the lips of a ten-year-old. "No," I said, "they won't kill us. We're protected by a very important man." (I did not mention Selim Bey's name because I was afraid that she had heard the same stories I had heard and would not know that he was a man who could be trusted.) "He won't let them hurt you. I promise."

She did not respond.

"Do you believe me?" I asked, a little anxiously, for more than anything in the world I did not want her to be afraid.

"Yes," she said in a small voice.

As an offer of friendship, I took a piece of bread from my tray and gave it to her. I watched her eat, her head bowed a little to hide her face. Although she must have been ravenous, she took only small bites and chewed daintily with her mouth closed, the way her parents must have taught her. For an instant I glimpsed the little girl they had known, the child whose hands were folded prettily on her school desk, who whispered secrets to her brother and sister at the dinner table. When she finished the bread, she picked the crumbs off her hand and touched them with her tongue.

"Will they feed us again?" she asked.

I nodded, and looked at the crack of light coming through the door frame. "Usually it's darker when dinner comes. When was the last time you ate?"

"Three days ago," she said.

Three days! She was nearly starving. "They'll feed you here," I said. "You'll eat so much your stomach will get big like mine." I patted my stomach and she smiled. She looked in the direction of the stalls where the horses were kept, though I do not think she saw them. She looked very tired, her eyes clouded by whatever had happened to her parents, to her home, to her shoes and ankles and the side of her face.

Dusk came next, then dinner.

I had been looking forward to this meal, knowing that it would go further toward restoring her spirits than all the promises I could make. For some reason, however, the soldier only brought one tray of food, and Seranoush and I shared it in silence, and I knew that whatever had happened to her had made her mistrustful even of me. Only time would prove to her that I was her friend, that I could be trusted. I did not know then that we had no time.

After dinner I turned off one of the lamps, and soon after that Seranoush drew one of my blankets over her and fell asleep almost immediately. I lay down a few feet from her and watched her fretful face gradually dissolve into a child's face. I wanted to kiss her cheek as I would have kissed Oskina's or Armenouhi's. I wanted to take her hand in mine and heal her bruised cheek and give her beautiful clothes. I wanted her to know that she was safe, that she was no longer alone, that this was not just the best day of my life but the best day of hers, as well. She had a family now. She had a brother, a father, and a best friend. I closed my eyes and thought about the governor, and my heart swelled with affection. Somehow Selim Bey had known that I was lonely, and somehow he had saved this girl and had her brought to me. Now she and I were not alone; we would never be alone again.

I was still awake when the door opened and the soldier came in. I was awake when the soldier held the lamp over my face, then Seranoush's. And I was awake when the soldier pulled the blanket off Seranoush's body and she screamed and he hit her across the face and pulled down his trousers. It was as if a kind of storm had suddenly ripped away the walls and roof of the stable and set upon Seranoush with a violence that cannot be imagined. And it must have been that same storm that swept me up and threw me at the soldier, my fists pulling at the back of his uniform with more strength than I possessed, my hands tearing at his face and throat with rage I had never known. I did not even see the hand that struck me, or the face that turned to me an instant before I was struck again, the side of my face stinging and blood in my mouth. I sprang again at the soldier, my arms around him, and this time the man exploded in my arms and I was on my back several feet away and unable to swallow or to breathe.

Three soldiers came to the stable that night, and the third soldier did not have to slap Seranoush or cover her face because she did not make a sound. She did not speak the next day, and she ate only a bite or two of the food I gave her. When I spoke to her, she gave no sign that she heard me. She pulled the blanket around her shoulders and turned away from me, from the world. And every night for seven nights, the soldiers took her outside and raped her.

On the morning of the eighth day, I called softly to her, but she did not answer. I leaned close to her and touched her face. Two soldiers carried her body out of the stable.

For many days I saw nothing in that stable but her face, heard nothing but her screams. I no longer groomed the horses or threw rocks at the target or tried in any way to pass the time. I no longer cared.

When Selim Bey finally came to see me, I told him what the soldiers had done. I thought he would be outraged, that he would want to find the men responsible and have them hanged or shot.

He listened, his arms folded across his chest, and when I finished, he looked genuinely puzzled.

"What do you care what happens to a little girl you do not know, who is nothing to you?" he said. "Do you know how many little girls there are in Turkey? Do you care what happens to every one of them— in all the stables in the world?"

"But you brought her here to be with me," I said.

"No. She was brought here for the soldiers, not for you."

I looked at him then as I might have looked at my

father if he had struck me. But the face I saw was not my father's, it was the face of Selim Bey, the Horse-shoer of Bashkale.

"Pick your friends carefully and protect them if you can," he said. "Leave the rest to their fate."

Chapter Twenty-one

One week later, I left for Andreas (the home of Selim Bey's father) with a Turkish soldier and a civilian. The governor told me that he would follow in a week or two, but I didn't care; I was no longer under his spell.

I sat sullenly beside the soldier, not wanting to speak or be spoken to. He was a young man with a handsome face, lazy black eyes, and the self-satisfied expression of one who had never needed more than a smile to get by. He kept a lit cigarette in his mouth at all times, and in his pocket he carried a gold watch that he consulted every hour or so for no other reason, it seemed, than to see it shine in the sun. His movements as he guided the horses were unhurried and economical, and occasionally he would raise his handsome face to the sky, close his heavy-lidded eyes, and grin at the sun as though all bets were down and he were holding a royal flush.

His name was Tovar, and he came from Tiflis,

where his father still made shoes. "The best in Turkey," he said. "One pair will last you your whole life." Then, with a shrug, he dismissed the subject. "You and the governor are friends?"

I did not answer.

"I like him," he said. "He doesn't give too many orders. Some of them tell you to do this, go there, just to hear themselves talk."

I was struck by his relaxed and friendly tone, and I had to remember that under different circumstances he might be ordering me out of my house, or shooting four boys by the bank of a river, or slapping Seranoush across the face as he pulled down his pants. Whether he was guilty or innocent, I did not trust him, and I had nothing to say to him or to any Turkish soldier. I wanted only to travel in silence to Andreas and be left alone.

"What do you think of this war?" he asked me.

"I don't like it," I said curtly.

He whistled and nodded his head. "You said it. What do we want to fight the Russians for? All they have in Russia is snow, and we have all the snow we need right here. We should attack a warmer country with beautiful women. Have you ever seen a Russian woman?"

I hadn't.

He shook his head. "I wouldn't fight a war for one," he said.

The civilian smiled, showing crooked black and brown teeth. He was a middle-aged man with soft brown eyes, and he chewed on a seemingly endless supply of nuts and dried apricots that he kept in his coat pocket. I might have believed in those soft eyes a year ago, but now I wondered what they hid. It was terrible to know how many things a human being could hide, and it explained my father's face and many of his expressions. I could feel my own mouth compressed like his against my desire to believe and to trust, and I wondered who had fooled him when he was young.

"You come from Kars?" the soldier asked me.

"Bitlis," I said.

"How are the women there? Beautiful?"

I nodded.

"The women in Tiflis are beautiful." He shook his head. "What do we need Russia for?" Then, with a shrug, he dismissed the subject, raised his face to the sun, and in no time was smiling at another winning hand.

Five days later we came to the walled city of Erzerum. We stopped at two abandoned Armenian homes, from which the soldier and civilian plundered all our wagon could hold.

Eight days later, we reached the mountain village of Andreas. The wagon stopped in front of a large two-story house, enclosed by a low stone wall. Just beyond the wall, an old man in a military uniform was inspecting a tomato in his garden, two small piles of fresh, very strong-smelling manure at his feet. This, I assumed, was Selim Bey's father. Without looking up, the old man dismissed the wagon with a wave of his hand and said, "In the back."

An Armenian servant and her son helped the soldier and the civilian unload the wagon while a young woman watched with an arrogant eye. Obviously, this was *her* home, these were *her* servants, and the valuables being unloaded were her tribute. I noticed that the woman servant walked with her head slightly bowed, and that once, when she accidentally brushed against the young woman, she bowed her head even lower and apologized not once, but twice. The young woman raised her chin a millimeter in reply, her gaze fixed on two silver trays that the civilian was carrying to the back door.

Finally, with a voice as superior as the tilt of her chin, she introduced herself to me as "the wife of General Khalil." She pointed at the old man, who still seemed to be examining the same tomato. "That is the general," she said. If she had said, "That is our gardener, he has recently lost his mind," I would not have been surprised.

"The Armenian sleeps in the stable!" the general called to his wife in a surprisingly strong voice.

She did not respond.

"Did you hear me!"

"Yes, Effendi," she said.

"In the stable!"

Chapter Twenty-two

For the first four days I never left the stable. Though I was still under Selim Bey's protection, I did not want to give General Khalil and his wife any reason to be displeased with me. I was an Armenian, and in Turkey anything could happen to an Armenian for any reason or for no reason at all. And so I would wait—for what was next, for each day to pass, for a year of days to pass and become the day when I could walk out of this stable, out of all the stables in Turkey, and reclaim my life.

The summer heat was debilitating, so I sat in the coolest corner I could find and swatted away the flies and watched the lizards come and go as they pleased. During the day I'd look through the spaces between the wood plank walls at the field behind the stable. I watched the cows nap in the summer heat and felt the minutes pass like a dry scentless breeze.

My meals of bread and broth were brought to me by the Armenian woman who had helped unload the wagon. Her name was Mrs. Mahari, and she came from Van, where her husband and older son had been killed. She had lost everything, yet there was nothing bitter or self-pitying about her. Only her eyes, the saddest I have ever seen, betrayed her. They were the eyes of Armenia, eyes no words could console.

She told me one day that she had worked for General Khalil for five months. Her voice lowered perceptibly when she said his name. She looked behind her at the doorway, where no one stood, then took a step toward me. "You must be very careful with him," she said, or, rather, whispered. "He's a little . . ." She tapped her forehead.

"Crazy?"

She put her finger to her lips. "Do what he tells you to do," she said. "If he asks you a question, nod or shake your head. But never speak to him. Only his wife is allowed to speak to him. And don't go near his garden."

"Is he crazy?" I whispered, somewhat urgently.

"Just do what he tells you. If you are sitting down when he comes to see you, stand up, but not too tall. Do you know what I mean?"

"No," I said.

"Be humble. Bow forward a little, narrow your shoulders. You're a servant now, and you must learn to think like a servant and behave like a servant at all times. Don't ever let them see who you really are or what you really think. You must use this," she touched her head.

"What do I do if he asks me a question I can't answer by nodding or shaking my head?"

"He won't," Mrs. Mahari said.

"What if he does?"

Mrs. Mahari looked at my tray. "If you want more food, tell me, and I'll see what I can do."

"Is his wife crazy, too?"

Mrs. Mahari smiled indulgently. "I'm not telling you this to frighten you," she said. "Just remember to use your head."

But that was no comfort, and after she left, the stable seemed a stranger and more sinister place, and its walls seemed to press upon me with the force of my own fears. I imagined all the things that General Khalil could do to me, the dozen different ways I could be killed or tortured. I got to my feet and stood with my back slightly bent and my head slightly bowed. I practiced nodding and shaking my head humbly, unemphatically. I walked humbly from one end of the stable to the other, all the time wondering what would happen to me if I stood too tall, or if I accidentally answered a question with my voice instead of my head. Dismissal? Arrest? Execution?

In retrospect, I am glad General Khalil came to the stable the next morning instead of a week or two weeks later. My imagination had already been fired, and if I had had to wait too long I might have died of anticipation.

I was sitting in my usual corner, finishing my breakfast, when the door opened and I saw his frail form. I froze for a moment, as though death or doom itself had found me, and then I was on my feet, shoulders stooped, head slightly bowed, heart pounding. Then, realizing that I was still standing too tall, I bent my knees a little.

As the old man limped into the stable, I retreated a step, so that my back was now literally against the wall. In the garden he had seemed harmless enough, contemplating his favorite tomato in a uniform he had not filled out in twenty years. Up close, however, there was a fierceness about him that was very nearly terrifying. He stood stiffly, at a slight forward tilt, apparently only a light breeze away from falling forward and breaking into a thousand pieces. The creased, ancient face, the features of which had long ago been claimed by wrinkles, wore an expression of extreme distaste brought about, I suppose, by having to enter a stable and address an Armenian. I realized then that I was looking directly at him, so I lowered my eyes.

"I don't know why my son wants you here," he said, "but you are not my guest. There are no Armenian guests on my property. Only servants. Do you understand? Nod your head."

I nodded. His voice, as craggy and decrepit as the rest of him, was still strong enough to carry across the stable and send a shiver up my spine.

He pointed an arthritic finger at me. "Don't go near my garden," he said. "If I find one of my tomatoes missing, I'll cut out your stomach to find it. I've killed Armenians before—men and boys. Nod your head."

I nodded.

"I want you to take my cows to the river every day. Wash them. Let them drink."

I was not sure if I should nod without being told to, so I just stared humbly at his knees.

"Do you hear me?"

I nodded.

"Do you know cows? Do you know how to take care of them?"

I nodded.

"Every day," he said.

The next morning, with a sense of dread, I did as I'd been told. I returned to the stable late in the afternoon, praying that I would not see General Khalil and he would not see me. I sat on the cement floor, listening for the old man's footsteps, afraid that if I made a sound he would know and come for me ("I've killed Armenians before—men and boys"). I would like to have dismissed him as a harmless old man who frightened children because he could no longer fight wars, but behind his threats, behind his presence, behind the sound of his voice, was the proof of sudden senseless violence, the proof of Seranoush, of Diran and Tavel and my grandmother.

As the days passed, I found myself sitting in the stable fearful that I had unknowingly crossed some imaginary line and that my punishment was limping toward me. I walked humbly, with my head bowed, even when the old man and his wife were not in sight. In dreams I found myself standing in the center of his garden, frozen with fear, trying to explain to him why I had touched one of his tomatoes. I was afraid even to look at his garden, afraid to utter a word, afraid that his eyes and ears were everywhere. I knew now why Mrs. Mahari had not spoken above a whisper, and why she had apologized so abjectly when she brushed against "the wife of General Khalil." She was terrified. And now, so was I.

Every afternoon when I returned from the field, I saw her and her son beating the rugs or emptying the chamber pots or risking a moment to rest and gaze at the mountains that bordered the village. We nodded or smiled when we saw one another, but we were afraid to speak. Still, their presence was a comfort to me. It was good to have my own people near me, to know that I was not completely alone.

And then, one afternoon, I did not see them, and my dinner was brought to me by a woman I did not know. Assuming she was Armenian, I asked her in our language where Mrs. Mahari and her son were, but the woman did not seem to understand. I asked her the same question in Turkish, and, in Turkish, she replied that she did not know any Mrs. Mahari. There *was* no Mrs. Mahari.

"She was here yesterday," I said. "She's been here for five months."

"*I* was here yesterday," the woman said. "No one else."

The next morning I went to the little house behind the stable, but Mrs. Mahari and her son were not there. There was no sign of them anywhere. They were gone.

And they would not have run away. There was nowhere to go.

I walked slowly, numbly, to the field, certain that they were dead, that for reasons of his own, the old man had had them killed or arrested, and that I was next. Five hours later I returned to the stable, where I waited for a meal I would be too nervous and too frightened to eat.

I sat stiffly against the back wall, listening for footsteps. When the Turkish woman brought my tray, I stared at the food as though it were poison. I ate a piece of bread (sniffing it and inspecting it first) and waited for the hours to pass, for the old man and his wife to get into bed, turn out their lamp, and fall into a deep unsuspecting sleep. There was still time to change my mind, time to get under my blankets and close my eyes and pretend that I was safe. But I knew what was possible in the world, and I could not let myself feel safe.

I had taken the precaution of arming myself with a pitchfork and a hammer. If the door opened and the old man stepped inside, I would either run him through with the pitchfork or crack open his withered pink skull with the hammer. I was prepared to do it. I hoped I would not have to, but I was prepared. I thought I heard his footsteps a dozen times, and every sound, real or imagined, made my heart jump.

When I thought enough time had passed, I folded my two blankets, took the last piece of bread from my tray, and slowly, slowly opened the stable door and crept into the night. Even as I was doing it, it did not feel real to me. It felt like a dream or something someone else was doing.

It was a clear, warm, windless night, far more welcoming than the one I had imagined. The sky was brilliant with stars, and the moon, nearly full, made a good light. The windows of the house were black, and there was no sound, save for the crickets. I waited for my eyes to adjust to the darkness; then, as quietly as I could, I followed the dirt path to the old man's garden, where I could see his precious tomatoes growing plump on the vine. I reached out and picked one, smelled its ripeness, placed it between my palms, and pressed until it burst in my hands. I quickly picked four or five others, pocketed two, and threw the rest into the night. I picked another, bit into it, chewed its firm, sweet meat, and set it down carefully in the soil where the old man would be sure to see it.

Chapter Twenty-three

I walked quickly through the satiny summer air, feeling almost buoyant. I had been so quiet and so careful for so many weeks that it was a relief to be free, to make noise when I walked, to kick up the dirt if I liked and imagine General Khalil's pinched old face when he saw his denuded vines.

Unfortunately, as the road rose and fell, wound through the little village of Andreas and beyond to flat blue fields, the novelty of freedom wore off, and as hour succeeded hour my pace slowed, until finally I became a plow horse trudging silently through the night with my sore feet and sweaty hide. I looked down at my feet and counted my footsteps. By my calculations, it would take twenty-seven thousand of them to reach Sivas, the nearest city.

Six or seven or eight miles into my journey, I sat down by the side of the road and rested. I reached into my pocket for the bread. I was hungry enough to eat it all, to eat all the bread and cheese and lamb and pastry in the world, but I stopped after two bites: For all I knew, there was no bread in Sivas; for all I knew, the bread in my hand was all the bread left in the world.

I was very tired and I closed my eyes, but I would not let myself sleep. I was my own father now, my own older brother telling myself that it was not safe to sleep, reminding myself how vulnerable a sleeping boy could be. I felt as though I had been walking all my life, from the moment Diran and Tavel were shot, a hundred years ago, to this very moment. And I knew that I could lie here for a hundred years more and never regain my strength. I could sleep for a hundred years and still be weary.

When I opened my eyes, the sky had changed color and I knew that it would soon be dawn. I stood up and began to walk.

And then, abruptly, I stopped. Far ahead, where the road curved, I saw the dark line of what looked like a funeral procession. I watched the line move, wondering if they were Armenian deportees. Then, thinking that my mother and Oskina might be among them, I began to walk again, faster than before. I began to run.

———

When I was two or three hundred yards away, I stopped.

I could see the carts moving slowly alongside the prisoners. I began to run again, and when I stopped I saw the horses and the dust raised by the carts. I expected to hear the same cries I had heard on the march to the river, but I heard only the creaking of the cart wheels as they turned, and I saw no soldiers, either behind or alongside the prisoners.

I realized then that they were Turks, not Armenians—refugees, not prisoners. (In those days, bands of Turkish refugees would walk for days or weeks toward the rumor of remote villages safe from the war.)

I was only a hundred yards from the back of the line, close enough to be seen, but I did not stop walking. I had well imagined the beggar's life that awaited me in Sivas, and it was clear to me that I had nothing to lose. There was only one problem: My accent was Armenian, and for that they might kill me.

I reached the back of the line, where sun-stained, leathery old women walked, most with their heads down, following the steps of those directly ahead of them. I slowed my pace a little so that I would not move up the line too quickly. I could feel my strangeness among them, and I was certain that they felt it, too, that something about my face or the way I walked told them that I was an Armenian. But they were too preoccupied by the rigors of walking to notice who had been added to or subtracted from their numbers. They had their own lives, their own losses to occupy their minds, and I was only one more body, young or old it did not matter; I had lost something, or everything, and so I was one of them.

I tried not to look at anyone, to keep my face expressionless, my eyes blank. Slowly, I became a part of the sound and movement, and I began to feel almost anonymous within it. I walked anonymously for what seemed like days.

"Who are you?" a man's voice said.

The question was directed at me, but I did not look up or alter my pace a step.

The man repeated the question, but I did not answer, and my face remained expressionless.

"What's wrong with you?" he said, so loudly that several heads turned. He pushed me, and I looked at him uncomprehendingly.

"Who are you?" he said.

I stared at him, pointed at my mouth, and shook my head.

"Mute?" he said. "Mute?"

I stared at the man, and he nodded. "Deaf and

mute," he said to the woman walking beside him. He patted my shoulder. "Forgive me," he said.

That evening, I sat with the others by the side of the road. My gaze fixed on the ground before me, I ate my own bread and tomatoes, and the rice and cubes of dried lamb that some of the older women had given me. All had approached me humbly, their heads bowed, the bowls of food resting on the palms of their hands. They bowed as I took the food and bowed again before they walked away. I did not know it then, but in their eyes, in the eyes of all Turks, the physically or mentally infirm were friends of God and therefore deserving of such kindness. As long as they believed I could not hear them or speak a single word, I would be safe.

The next day we left the road to Sivas and climbed a mountain road that led to a small village of low, mud-brick dwellings bleached gray by the sun. There were many refugees already living in the village: women mending clothes or kneading dough for bread, men chopping wood, children pouring madzoon into jars or watching their grandmothers knit socks or vests from the wool of the sheep that grazed beside a donkey in the field beyond the village.

This was my new home, and these men, women, and children, many of whom shared an unalterable and unreasoning hatred of all Armenians, were my new family.

I walked with my head bowed, my fear creating a wall between myself and the sights and sounds of the village. I spread my blankets on the ground and looked at the low, brown mountains in the distance. I had never felt more alone in my life.

Chapter Twenty-four

At first I lived in great fear—even in my dreams I was afraid to speak. I did nothing spontaneously or haphazardly. Every glance, every turn of my head was thought out in advance and deliberately executed. Inside myself I spoke aloud, I sang or screamed or cried, but the face I presented to my fellow villagers was always the same. I saw them, at first, as a mob of antagonists that I neither liked nor trusted. Man or woman, young or old, they were the same in my eyes. Those who had lived in the village longest inhabited the mud dwellings, with interiors that boasted rug-covered earthen floors and two or three pieces of furniture. Others lived in tents of black goat-hair cloth, and the rest slept on woolen mattresses under worn blankets or comforters. During the day, all were busy with one thing or another: milking the goats, churning butter, hunting for food, or gathering together in religious worship.

"Come to prayer!" the muezzin cried early in the morning. "Prayer is better than sleep!"

I observed their religious ceremonies with interest—the chants, the prostrations and prayers for protection and blessings, and my heart was softened by what I saw. "God is great!" the muezzin proclaimed to the congregation. "Thee only do we worship, to Thee do we cry for help." I had never witnessed an Islamic service before, and found it, in spirit, not very different from the church services that my family and I had attended every Sunday in Bitlis. The faces in worship were the same, the hope and pain and devotion in their eyes was the same, and in their hearts, as in mine, lived the same longing for a better world and a better life.

Gradually, as my own voice grew quiet within me, I was able to distinguish from the seventy or eighty villagers certain names, certain faces, certain traits that separated them—the eyes of one, the laughter of another, a gesture of compassion or humility. There was Kiazim, small, with violent eyes, who hunted with his younger brother, Reshid. There was Mustafa, who killed the sheep; and Shirin, Mustafa's daughter, who sheared the sheep and gave them names. There was Sait, who made faces for me to laugh at; and Yakup, who spoke with great energy and humor; and

Aziz, who taught me how to tend the sheep; and Ahmet, Aziz's brother, who liked to drink wine and fire his rifle at the sky.

At night I ate with them before the fires and listened to the stories they told. They talked about their lives before the war, about a sister or brother who had been killed, about the men and great beasts they had slain. All but one was convinced that I was deaf and mute, and Mustafa, dark lined face, sharp black eyes, and heavy gray brows, would never be convinced. It was Mustafa who walked over to me my first day in the village and squeezed my ear so hard that I screamed. It was Mustafa who kicked me when he called my name, the name they had given me, and I did not answer. He looked at me and his eyes said he knew: knew my parents were dead, knew I was Armenian, knew I should be dead. At night, by the fires, he cursed the Armenians and said that the war would be over if the Turkish army had not been betrayed in Van. His two sons had been killed by the Russian army, but he blamed the Armenians, "the infidels" he called them. I made it my business to stay as far away from him as possible, hoping that in time he would either accept me or forget about me.

Most of my days were spent in the field, watching

the sheep and the donkey. Sometimes Yakup and Sait would join me, and we would play the pebble game of Gap. The name they gave me was Galib, and as the weeks and months passed, I became more and more willing to think of myself as Galib, to see the village through Galib's eyes and hear only the silence inside myself. And, as Galib, it was not hard for me to think of the village as my home, or to see in each face something that reminded me of the faces of my own friends and family. In Sait I sometimes saw Pattoo; in Aziz I saw Tavel; and in Reshid I saw Manoosh. In Shirin I saw no one I had ever known, but I liked her face most of all. I had hardly noticed her when I first came to the village, but soon I found myself watching her, wondering what she was thinking. It seemed to me that she was as much a stranger in the village as I, for she spent most of her time alone, rarely speaking to the others. Though she was only sixteen or seventeen years old, her black hair was graying, and her eyes were as dark and knowing as a woman twice her age. If she had had anyone but Mustafa for a father, she might have been happy, but he was as much her curse as he was mine. Still, she remained a dutiful daughter: She served him his meals, sat beside him while he ate, bore his insults when he drank, and did not cry or make a sound when he struck her. But she kept her heart to herself.

The rains that summer were as gentle as a mother's kiss—sweetening the air, ripening the soil, and refreshing the soul and the senses. In the daytime, I heard the echoes of gunfire in the forest; at night, I feasted on many kinds of meat. Aziz put his arm around me one evening and said, "This is my son." Shirin smiled at me. When I looked at her, she turned away. Kiazim took me hunting. He did not tell me what we were hunting for, but when we returned he announced to the others that I was a born hunter. Sait had fever and spoke wildly for many days. I liked Sait and was afraid he would die. In his delirium he placed a hand on my shoulder and said "my friend" over and over until I thought I would cry. I prayed for him to recover. I prayed in Armenian and Turkish, so that God would be sure to hear me, and when he recovered I embraced him as I might have embraced Pattoo. At night I no longer dreamed about my family.

One day while I was looking after the sheep, I heard footsteps behind me. This was not unusual. Sometimes Yakup or Sait would sneak up behind me and try to scare me by covering my eyes, but I always heard them, and I was always ready. And I was ready now, for one or the other—and also for Mustafa, who never left my mind for a moment. But it was Shirin who sat down beside me, and when I saw her all my breath seemed to leave my body. I looked at her, feeling my face redden, and she smiled. I turned from her and watched the clouds drift across the sky. Shirin looked at the clouds. If at that moment she had asked me who I was, I would have told her. If she had asked me if I was Armenian, I would have said yes. I would have told her anything. But she did not say a word.

She began to sing softly, to herself. I listened, looking at the brown hills beyond the field. I closed my eyes and imagined that she was singing for me, that the warm wind on my face was the breath of her song. I wondered if she would have sat with me if she had known that I was not deaf. I wondered if she would have sung for me if she had known that I was Armenian. I wanted to look at her, but I was afraid that she would see in my eyes that I could hear her. But I had to look at her, and when I did, she stopped. And smiled.

"I'm not talking," she explained. "I'm only singing."

I looked at her curiously.

"Singing," she said. And then she sighed. "I wish you understood."

I understand, my mind said.

"No, I don't," she said. "I'm glad you don't under-stand."

Far away, I heard Mustafa's voice calling her, but she did not answer or even turn her head.

"Shirin!" The voice was closer now, but still she did not answer.

I waited. Finally, I heard his footsteps behind us.

"You are not a shepherd, Shirin," Mustafa's voice said. "Leave that to him."

After dinner that evening, Mustafa stood up, his face flushed with wine, his belly tight with food, and began to dance. Kiazim joined in, then Aziz and Sait. Soon all the men were dancing. Kiazim took off his shirt and made great circles with it as he danced. The other men did the same, while their women watched and laughed and clapped. I had never seen such dancing or heard such laughter in my life, and I wanted to join in, wanted to stand and dance and clap with the others. One of the men reached out to Shirin, but she shook her head. Then she looked across the fire at me.

That night, I lay under my blankets and thought about her. I told her that I was Armenian and she said that she knew.

"How?"

"I know you," she said. "The same way you know me."

I told her that she was beautiful, and she shook her head. "Only to you," she said. "Only for you."

I looked at the moon and wondered if she was looking at the same moon, her thoughts answering mine. I could hear the few remaining revelers in the distance, drunk sounding and fraternal, and I fell asleep to their voices.

I do not remember what I dreamed, only that I was suddenly awake. Something heavy shifted on the grass beside my head. I listened, but heard only the crickets and the wind.

"Galib!" a voice whispered. "Galib!"

It was Mustafa.

"Open your eyes, my friend. I won't hurt you."

I felt his face close to mine, his breath hot and sour with wine.

"No one is going to hurt you, my friend. I only want you to open your eyes so we can talk. You must be tired of your game by now."

He was leaning over me. I felt his knee against the back of mine and a cold sweat collecting on my chest and under my arms. It took all my concentration to keep my body still and my breathing deep and rhythmical.

"You can make fools of the others, Galib, but you cannot make a fool of me. I am not a fool, Galib. I have eyes, and they see who is lying and who is telling the truth."

Even with my eyes closed I could feel him watching me, searching my face for some sign that I heard him.

"Your family is dead," he said. "I know that. My family is dead, too. My sons are dead. My name is dead. But listen to me, Galib—your name will die, too. Do you hear me, Armenian? Your name will die, too."

The next day I was left alone to watch the sheep. Sait had asked if he could stay with me, and Mustafa told him he could not. It was a hot day, so I tied the donkey's rope around my leg so that he would not lead the sheep to the shade of the rocks or to the hills beyond the field.

I was sitting on the grass, my back against a rock. I had been too frightened to sleep the night before, and now my eyes were heavy and the wind and the warm sun were like a blanket. I closed my eyes and opened them. I closed my eyes and slept.

And then someone was kicking me.

"Where are the sheep?" Mustafa said.

I opened my eyes and saw that the donkey and the sheep were gone. Twenty or thirty others were looking at the grass where the sheep had been—talking loud and fast, pointing beyond the rocks, pointing beyond the trees. In every face there was fear.

Mustafa pulled me up to my feet. "Where are the sheep, boy?" He was smiling.

I looked at him.

"You fell asleep, eh?" He turned to Sait, who was watching helplessly. "Find the sheep," he said. The villagers had scattered in every direction, whistling for the sheep, calling the donkey. Only Mustafa stayed behind. The sun was low in the sky.

"That was a stupid thing to do, my friend." He clapped his hands and swung hard into my belly. I dropped to my knees, all the air gone from my body. Mustafa's boot flashed toward my face and missed. I tried to stand, and he kicked out and caught me on the side of the head. He pulled me up by my hair and brought his knee up between my legs.

"Did you think you could fool me?" he said. He clasped his hands and brought them down on my back like a sledgehammer. He kicked and missed, kicked again and caught me in the ribs. "Did you think you could fool a Turk?"

I tried to roll away, and my head was stung. And then I saw the blood—beads and tracks of blood. I swam up to my feet and my head was blown back and I heard a crack and I knew that my nose was broken. I felt something sharp in my ribs, in my back—three, four, five blows—thump, thump thump, like drums. Again I tried to stand, and again I was blown back, my face in the dirt. From far away: "You cannot make a fool of me."

Later that night the others returned with the sheep and the donkey. Not one sheep had been lost. I lay on my back, far from the fires. Sait and Shirin had brought me food, but I would not eat. Shirin tried to sit beside me, but I waved her away. I did not want anyone to see me. I closed my eyes and felt every punch and every kick. I ran my tongue over my teeth and felt the ones that were loose. I did not touch my nose because I knew it was broken. I was glad that my mother and father could not see me now. For the first time in many months, I did not know what would become of me. I knew I should leave, but I did not know where to go. Without this village, I would have no home. I would have streets to beg on and roads where the dead were not buried. I would have my tongue, but who would I speak to? I was afraid to leave, and I hated my fear. My father never would have lived among his enemies. But my father was dead and the unknown went on forever. The unknown filled the sky and darkened the far trees and the world beyond them. Perhaps someday I would speak to the villagers and they would not kill me. Perhaps someday I could laugh at Yakup's stories and tell Shirin she was beautiful. And wasn't Sait my friend? They were all my friends, and Mustafa could not hate me forever. I looked deep into the night, half hoping to see my father's eyes.

I raised my head and saw that the fires were gone. Slowly, I turned on my side and tried to stand. "No," a voice said, and I felt a hand on my shoulder. It was Shirin. I raised my hand to wave her away, and she took my hand and held it. "Rest," she said.

Gradually my wounds healed. My nose was still fat, but it did not hurt so much when I touched it. As time passed I no longer thought about leaving. I told myself that the village was my home. I was certain that Mustafa was finished with me: It was as though all his hate had gone into beating me, and now he was empty. He ate in silence and drank alone. Sait carved me a knife. We threw rocks at targets and made faces in the dirt with our knives. He cut our names in a tree and said we were brothers. Shirin no longer came to the field. At dinner we sat on opposite sides of the fire, and when I looked at her, she shook her head slightly, and I knew that Mustafa had forbidden her to talk to me.

One afternoon, Sait and I were playing Gap on the dirt path that separated the field from the dwellings of the village. I was winning, and Sait had become so quiet that I knew that he was only a minute or two away from forfeiting.

He picked up the pebbles, tossed them in the air, and caught three on the back of his hand. I picked up the pebbles, tossed them in the air, and caught six. I waited for Sait to write down the score, but he was not looking at me. He was looking past me, and his expression had changed. I turned and saw the soldiers. There were two of them walking up the mountain road, their rifles slung over their shoulders. The bearded man between them had no shirt, and his pants were torn and bloody. He had many wounds on his body, and the wounds were packed with dirt. His face was crusted with dirt and blood, and his arms hung loosely at his sides. He fell to his knees, and the soldiers dragged him until he found his feet again.

The villagers began to talk among themselves. I heard "Armenian" many times and felt something sickening stir inside me. I looked at the man's pants and I could see that they had been made from fine material. I tried to meet the man's eyes, but his eyes met nothing. He must have been hiding in the mountains for months. Mustafa whispered something to Kiazim, and

Kiazim nodded, still watching the soldiers. I looked at Sait helplessly, as I would have looked at Sisak or Pattoo, but Sait shrugged his shoulders as if to say, "It's only an Armenian."

The villagers gathered twenty or thirty feet from the soldiers and their prisoner. I searched for Shirin, who was standing well behind the others. I saw her turn and walk quickly toward the field. One of the soldiers said something to Mustafa, and Mustafa nodded his approval. The other soldier tied the prisoner to a tree, walked a few feet away, and raised his rifle. The prisoner moved his lips but made no sound. He closed his eyes. The soldier aimed but did not shoot. The prisoner opened his eyes and began to shake. He looked at the soldier steadily.

"Shoot," he said in Armenian.

The soldier placed his finger on the trigger and waited.

"Shoot!" the prisoner said.

The soldier waited. Everyone was silent.

The prisoner began to beat the back of his head against the tree, and there was a shot and a crack and he was dead. The bullet had passed through his mouth.

That night I lay under my blankets, my eyes open. After the soldiers had taken the prisoner's boots, the children looked through his pockets, the bravest touching the hole at the back of his head and instantly recoiling. I remembered looking desperately from face to face, hoping to find some sign of grief or horror, but I had seen nothing: Mustafa had already turned away, and Kiazim was talking animatedly to the soldiers. Yakup sat beneath a tree and closed his eyes. And Sait—my brother, my best friend—Sait looked at the body quizzically and ran his tongue across his lips because they were dry. My throat had ached because I could not scream, and my head hurt because I could not cry. There was something thick and salty in my throat— something like hardened tears or rage that swelled whenever I swallowed. I prayed for the dead man's soul in Armenian, and hated the people I had thought were my friends. I remembered seeing all but Shirin, and believing all but Shirin would have killed me for what I was.

I was not Galib, and this was not my home and these people were not my family. I had known that the instant I heard the shot. And when the prisoner slumped forward, I saw my father and my brothers and myself. I had known then that I was leaving, that I had to leave.

It was late now, and I listened to the silence of the village. I folded my blankets, left the knife Sait had carved for me on the ground, and began to walk toward the spot where Shirin slept under a blanket outside her father's tent. I walked slowly, careful not to make a sound. I passed Reshid, Ahmet, Aziz. I could see Shirin now, lying beneath her blankets. I could hear Mustafa snoring inside his horsehair tent and feel my heart beating against my chest. I walked the last ten feet and looked at her sleeping face. I was afraid to touch her, afraid she would scream. I crouched beside her, knowing I did not have much time and that I was a fool to take such a chance. I touched her shoulder lightly, but she did not move. I touched her face, my hand ready to cover her mouth, and her eyes opened and she looked at me. I put my finger to my lips, and she nodded. I opened my mouth to speak, but made no sound. I leaned forward and pressed my lips against her cheek.

"Thank you," I whispered, first in her language, then in my own.

She sat up and I was on my feet. And then I was running.

BOOK THREE

Chapter Twenty-five

I had not realized how hard it would be to find my way down a mountain in the dark. I had not realized how many terrifying sounds the darkness could make or how treacherous a winding mountain road could be. Twice that night, I found myself a step away from a long, rolling fall to a broken leg, neck, or back. Finally, finally, I reached the bottom and began my long journey to Sivas. I knew nowhere else to go.

I was walking fast through the autumn cold, carrying my two blankets, staring at the road ahead, willing myself over every foot, every mile. I walked not as Galib, with my head bowed, but as myself, with my own face, my own determination.

I had not heard my voice aloud for three months, yet I had no desire to speak or to make a single sound. There was nothing to say, and at that moment my voice and all the words I knew seemed no more meaningful than the bark of a dog. I would never see Shirin again, and there was nothing I could say aloud that would change that. I wished I had said more to her; I wished I had told her my name; I wished I had told her she was beautiful. And now I was walking away from her, and we would live the rest of our lives apart, with only the sun and the moon in common. The years would pass and our faces would fade, become other faces, and our memories of each other would fade into other memories and we would not be sure what we had really felt and what we had only dreamed. All I would ever have of her were the few words she had spoken to me, her hand on my shoulder, her eyes across the fire. What difference did the sound of my voice make if I would never see Shirin again?

I was walking faster now, trying to outdistance this moment, to make it a part of the past, to hurry toward Sivas as though it were waiting to welcome me, as though it were not a city of smoke and rubble, broken glass and hungry dogs. And even if the city was populated and the buildings still stood, who would welcome an Armenian?

I entered Sivas a few hours after dawn. I walked up a wide street past alleys and empty stores, my heart growing heavier with each step. There were a few Turkish civilians on the street, a few lazy wagons rumbling over the cobblestone, but all in all, the city was no different from Bitlis and Erzerum and Kars. I walked up and down the smaller streets, now and then peering through the glass panes at bare wood floors and dusty sunlit counters. I entered what had once been an Armenian bakery and looked for food, but there wasn't any; there was only dust.

I walked out of the store and looked up and down the street, knowing there was nowhere to go. It did not matter how far I walked or in which direction, it would all be the same. And the next city would be the same, and on and on until I could go no farther. I should never have left General Khalil; I should never have left Shirin; and now all the wrong turns I had taken, all the wrong decisions I had made had brought me here.

I sat down on the street. There was nothing to do but spread my blankets on the ground, lie down, close my eyes, and try to sleep. I had come to the end of whatever resources I possessed.

From somewhere I heard: "You jackass! What's the matter with you? Like this! Like this!"

I looked up and down the street, unable to believe my ears. Someone was speaking Armenian! I ran down the street in the direction I thought the voice had come from, then ran the other way until I came to a coppersmith's shop, the only open store on the block. I entered the store and saw copper everywhere: copper plates, drums, bowls, and pots.

An old man was sitting on a chair, beating the rim of a copper pot with a small hammer. Beside him sat a boy who was polishing a copper plate. The old man and the boy looked at me, and I was afraid I had somehow made a mistake, that I was standing in the wrong shop, looking at the wrong people. I had an impulse to turn and run, but instead I said the first words that came to my mind.

"I am Armenian," I said, and the words sounded foreign to my ears.

The old man's expression did not change. "Where do you come from?" he asked, in *Armenian*, thank God.

"Bitlis."

"Bitlis? Bitlis is far, far away. How can you come from Bitlis?"

"I come from Bitlis," I said.

The old man studied my face. Then he stood up, and I realized I had been talking to a giant. He was at least six feet tall, and he must have weighed two hundred forty pounds. His arms, though bleached and softened by the years, were still the arms of a blacksmith, or at least a former blacksmith, and the wide chest and broad shoulders confirmed that he had once been a man of unnatural strength.

He closed the door, locked it, and sat down again. "Tell me your story," he said.

And I did. Without hesitation, in my own voice, my own language, free from Mustafa and General Khalil, from the danger of being noticed, of being heard, of being Armenian, I told him everything. The old man listened calmly, now and then patting the air to quiet me when my voice became too loud.

When I finished, he nodded thoughtfully and began to rub his mouth. "So the other cities are like Sivas," he said sadly. He reached for a pipe sitting in a holder on the table beside him, lit it, and puffed at it a few times.

"I am Ara Sarkisian," he said. "And this is Serop. His family was killed, too."

Serop smiled diffidently. He had black hair, huge brown eyes, and a comically large nose. Except for the nose, his features were fine, almost delicate. I noticed then that his feet were bare and that his bare legs were curiously undeveloped.

"There was also much bloodshed here," Ara Sarkisian said. "They took the men first, as you said, then the rest. But they didn't bother with me. I am an old man and I can shine their copper. And the boy, the boy was lucky."

His voice was calm, reassuring, with no hint of the lion I had heard roaring halfway down the street. He looked at me for a moment as though he was making up his mind about something.

"It will be safer for all of us if you stay in back," he said, motioning behind him. "I can't afford to keep this door closed all day."

The old man took me to a small room at the rear of the shop. The first thing I saw when I entered the room was a picture of Jesus Christ over one of the two beds. Then I noticed how neatly the beds were made, and the almost prim simplicity and spotlessness of the room itself. There were several books stacked on a bedside table, and on another small table were two candles, a pictureless wood frame, and an empty drinking glass. Beside the table was a straw basket, and on the floor was a plain cloth rug. There was nothing else—no mirrors, no scent of smoke, not even a stray sock or shoe. It was a modest room, the room of a priest or a penitent, a room as tidy as the shop beyond its door was disheveled, and I trusted the man who lived there. I knew he was taking a chance by letting me stay with him, and

I knew what would happen to him, to all of us, if I was discovered by the gendarmes.

I spent the next several hours listening to the banging of hammer on copper, thinking about Shirin, and trying unsuccessfully to sleep.

When the door finally opened, I saw Ara Sarkisian in the doorway with Serop in his arms. The old man carried the boy to one of the beds, laid him down gently, gave one of the lifeless legs a pat, and asked me what I wanted for dinner.

Before I could answer, he said, "If it is something other than rice and vegetables, you will have to eat somewhere else."

Serop laughed, and Ara Sarkisian looked at me. "He thinks that everything I say is funny. I call him a donkey and he laughs."

We ate on the floor in the small room. Although my surroundings were new, they were not strange to me, and I felt very much at home, as though I were sharing a meal with my grandfather and a favorite cousin. After dinner, we talked. I had assumed that Serop was Ara Sarkisian's grandson, but he wasn't. The coppersmith had found him lying in the street and carried him back to his shop. "The biggest mistake I ever made," he said, winking at me. "The boy has been nothing but misery from then until now. But I have a good heart, a generous soul, and a very soft head. Right?" he said, turning to the boy with mock ferocity.

Serop laughed delightedly and looked at me to see if I was enjoying the performance as much as he. The coppersmith continued: "Here is how it happened, exactly. I am walking down the street, minding my own business, as happy as an old man can be, when I see this boy lying in the middle of the street, hands behind his head, lazy as an aristocrat. Well, I think to myself, maybe I can help myself a little—teach the boy a trade, put him to work, take it easy in my old age." He shook his head ruefully. "How was I to know he was a donkey in boys' clothing? God Himself couldn't teach this boy a trade. I say, 'Hold the cloth like this and rub in circles'; he holds the cloth like this and rubs back and forth. I say, 'Hold the hammer like this and tap softly'; he holds the hammer like this and strikes like a blacksmith." He shrugged. "But I am a humble man. If this is the best God can do for me, who am I to complain?"

With mock solemnity he excused himself from the room, taking his empty glass with him. While he was gone, Serop whispered confidentially, almost apologetically, "He snores."

That was all he had time to say, because a moment

———

later Ara Sarkisian returned with two cloves of garlic and his glass half filled with raki. He offered me a clove, which I refused, ate a clove himself, raw, finished the raki in a gulp, and declared that it was time to go to sleep. After helping me make my bed in a corner of the room, he gently lifted Serop off the floor and set him down on his, Serop's, bed. Then, with great care, he pulled the sheet and comforter over the boy's body, tucked in the sides, kissed the boy's cheek, got into his own bed, and turned off the lamp. The room was silent.

I lay in the dark with my eyes open, feeling very fortunate to have found such a friend. Instead of shivering in some alley, nibbling whatever was left of the food I had begged for, I was in this warm room, my belly full, my heart content, my mind drifting toward a deep and satisfying sleep.

And then I heard a sound so loud and so unexpected that I sat up in my makeshift bed, afraid that someone was choking to death. A second later, there was another gutturalism as deafening as the first. I realized then that this was what Serop meant by "he snores," which, to my way of thinking, did not begin to describe what I was hearing.

It was without a doubt the loudest noise I had ever heard any man or any animal make in my life—six full feet and two hundred forty pounds of snoring. I covered my ears, but it didn't help. I said his name loudly, hoping to startle him out of his slumber, but he did not stir. I slapped the floor hard with the palm of my hand and cleared my throat several times. Nothing.

Just when I thought I would either have to leave the room or wake him up, he stopped. And Serop began to snore.

I stayed with Ara Sarkisian for eight days. I was confined to the back room, where I caught up on the sleep I had lost, and busied myself polishing copper drums and plates. Every night he drank two glasses of raki ("to settle the nerves"), ate a clove or two of garlic ("to strengthen the blood"), and talked to me quietly about his life. Being very young, I had assumed that old men had always been old, that the coppersmith had always polished and hammered copper, that the bachelor had never known love. I thought that Ara Sarkisian had always slept alone in that back room, always eaten rice and vegetables for dinner, and always snored ferociously. And so I was surprised to learn that he had lived half his life in Moosh and had wanted to be an artist when he was a young man. He showed me some of the pencil sketches he had done of a woman on a horse. I asked him if the woman was his wife, and he smiled.

"That woman comes from here," he said, pointing at his head. "This was my wife. He opened a drawer and handed me a photograph of a lovely woman with dark rings of curls and a very pleasing smile. When I commented on her beauty, he nodded gravely and put the photograph back in the drawer. I noticed that it fit the empty frame perfectly.

He told me he had been a strongman in his village, performing feats of strength on the street for money. He bent bars, wrestled two men at once, and held his own against three men in a tug of war. The bars, he said, had already been bent several times, so they were flexible, but the other feats were genuine.

"Shake my hand," he said.

I took his huge hand, and he slowly squeezed harder, and harder still, until I could feel the bones in my hand begin to give.

"I can squeeze much harder than that," he said, letting go. "How old do you think I am?"

"Fifty-five," I said diplomatically. He was probably sixty.

"I am seventy-four years old. When I was fifty-five I could still break open a melon with my hands. But time takes everything. Your home, your family, your work, your strength, the woman you love. Everything."

He smiled. "You are looking for a home, for a family. Do you know where your real home is? Your real home is here." He pointed at his heart. "Who you are and what you believe in is your real home, the only home no one can take from you, the only home that will last." He held up his hands. "There is nothing these hands can hold that is worth having. They cannot hold the moonlight, or the melody of a song, or even the beauty of a woman. They can touch her face, but not her beauty. Only the heart can hold such things.

"Time takes everything, Vahan. But your heart, your character, your faith, do not belong to time. So build your home here," he said, touching his chest. "And make that home strong, make that home beautiful. Then you will always be safe, and you will never be alone."

It was not my desire to leave Ara Sarkisian. I would have been proud to sit beside him in his shop, polishing and hammering copper and listening to a lifetime of stories, but the conditions in Turkey made such a choice impossible.

Every night after dinner he went for a walk and would not say where he had been when he returned. But I knew what he was looking for, and I found myself trying to memorize every detail of his shop—the oil stains on the table, the old newspapers on the floor, the smell of the polish, the brass knobs on the door—so that I could return to it, and him, someday, at least in my mind.

On the night of the eighth day, he told me we were going out. "I've found some people who I think can help you," he said.

"Who?"

"Who? Who? Are you an owl?" He turned to Serop. "This shop is yours until I return— alone, God willing. Try not to destroy it." Then, to me, "Come on, Who."

As we stepped outside and he closed the door of the shop behind him, his face became serious. "If there was any way I could keep you here with me, I would. You know that, don't you?"

"Yes," I said, and felt a sudden surge of affection that made it impossible to say more.

He nodded and patted my shoulder. "Let's take a walk."

The fog had set in, and the streets were damp and the autumn air was cold and heavy with mist. We walked quickly down the dark streets, hoping to get where we were going without running into any gendarmes. I began looking here and there for a suitable sidewalk to sleep on, for I had already decided that Ara Sarkisian had taken enough chances on my behalf and that I would leave him tomorrow whether or not I had a place to go. I would not allow myself to be a danger to him and Serop any longer.

Ahead I saw a white building that was almost identical to an American Mission in Bitlis. There was the same high white door, the same cross, the same windows. I followed my friend to the mission, wondering if it was really going to be my new home, and what kind of home it would be, and if I would be welcome there.

Ara Sarkisian knocked on the door, and we waited.

"Smile," he whispered. "You look like somebody owes you money."

I smiled.

"Good boy. Don't talk too much. These people like to do the talking. Just nod and smile and try to look pleasant."

He knocked again, and I looked at the door, half expecting to hear a voice tell us to go away.

But the door opened.

Silhouetted against the dim light of a hallway stood a stiff, spinsterish woman who gazed at the old man with moist, humorless eyes and whispered, "Come with me."

We followed her down the bare beige hallway (the walls of which seemed to grow higher as my nervousness mounted) to a closed door that said Eugenia Fauld. Mrs. Fauld shook our hands briskly and told us to sit down. She was a tall, immaculate, middle-aged woman with a slightly pointed chin and frank, intelligent eyes. She wore no jewelry, and she exuded an air of firmness and self-sufficiency that made it quite clear that she was the ultimate authority at the mission and that her good or bad opinion of me would seal my fate.

On the wall behind her chair were a Swiss flag and a white cross. I said a silent prayer to the cross and surreptitiously wiped my wet palms on the sides of my pants.

"Your friend has told me your story," Mrs. Fauld said to me. "You have no living relatives?"

"No," I said, remembering Ara Sarkisian's advice not to talk too much.

Mrs. Fauld nodded. "There's one problem," she said. "We have many Armenian orphans here, but they are all girls. The Turkish authorities have forbidden us to take any boys. If the authorities were to discover you here, the mission would be closed."

My heart sank. I assumed that the matter was settled, that there was nothing more for her to do but stand up, tell me how sorry she was, shake my hand, and wish me luck.

"I can give you a dress and shoes and stockings, and something to cover your hair," she said. "Would that be all right?"

I looked at Ara Sarkisian, then at Mrs. Fauld. "I can stay here?"

"If you like," Mrs. Fauld said.

"I would. I would like to very much."

Mrs. Fauld was silent for a moment. "It might work," she said, "for a little while, at least. Then we can see. We might even be able to find a home for you."

"Thank you," I said, secretly thrilled by the mention of the word *home*.

Ara Sarkisian thanked Mrs. Fauld for helping us. I turned to him, but I did not know what to say.

"You're welcome," he said, patting my shoulder. Then to Mrs. Fauld: "You're getting a very good boy here. You'll find he's worth the trouble."

The next morning, I put on the dress, the stockings, the scarf, and the shoes I had been given and looked at myself in the mirror on the wall beside my bed. At first I saw only myself, but when I squinted my eyes, I was the image of Oskina.

We had been told all our lives how greatly we resembled each other, and now she seemed truly to be looking back at me, about to smile, about to speak and tell me the secret of how she had survived. I told myself it was *my* reflection, yet I kept staring at her, almost believing that she was staring back at me. I said her name aloud, and for a moment, against all logic, I knew for certain she was alive, and then came a pain so strong that her image vanished and it was my own face looking back at me, my common sense insisting she was dead, the same as my mother and father and family. It was too foolish and too painful to imagine otherwise, knowing I could never find her. I turned away from the mirror resolving never to think such thoughts again.

Chapter Twenty-six

My new name was Verkine, and if I was ever questioned by an authority, I was to say that I came from Van, where my father had been a dressmaker. Because Mrs. Fauld did not want the other girls to know that I was a boy, I spent most of my time alone in my room. I ate my meals at the teachers' table, and I was allowed in the play area outside, alone, for one hour per day. Now and then some of the girls looked at me strangely, as though they sensed that something was amiss, but I do not think any of them guessed that I was a boy. I think, as far as they were concerned, I was merely a shy girl with large wrists, and a figure that might euphemistically have been called athletic.

"We're going to find a home for you very soon," Mrs. Fauld would assure me every two or three weeks. I wanted to believe her, for despite what Ara Sarkisian had said, I still wanted a home and a family more than anything in the world, but if I was honest with myself,

I had to admit that there was probably no such place and no such people. Therefore, when Mrs. Fauld called me into her office one morning, I could not guess what she wanted.

"Do you know how to milk a cow?" she asked me.

"Yes," I said, vaguely perplexed by the question.

"And take care of a horse?"

"I took care of Selim Bey's horses."

Mrs. Fauld allowed herself a rare smile. "An Armenian doctor is looking for a servant to help his wife. I've told Dr. Tashian—that's his name—all about you, and he wants to meet you. If he likes you, and I'm sure he will . . ."

She left the sentence unfinished. We both knew what she meant. If he liked me I would have a home.

"We leave this afternoon," she said. "Behind the mission."

Miss Lichtenstein, one of the teachers, cut my hair, and Mrs. Fauld gave me a brush to clean my fingernails, and a new bar of soap. I scrubbed my face hard and washed my ears and behind my ears and my neck and my fingernails, so that I would make the best impression possible.

An hour later, I was sitting beside Mrs. Fauld in a

taxi, so excited that I was barely able to keep still. As the taxi rolled away from the curb, I did not even glance back at the mission. All my thoughts centered around the life that awaited me. I had imagined that life so many times that I felt as though I were returning to a house I already knew, to a family I already loved. There was no question in my mind that I was exactly the kind of boy the doctor was looking for, yet, as the taxi rumbled down the street, I could not help wishing that I were a little taller, or perhaps three or four years older, with a broader back and bigger arms. And I could not help wondering what Mrs. Fauld would do with me if the doctor did not like me.

An hour later we reached the village of Gavra, in the northern part of Sivas. The taxi stopped in front of a beautiful brown and white house that was almost as big as my home in Bitlis. There was a gate in front of the house, and beyond the gate, I saw a flower garden, a great extravagance in those days. On the roof a German flag was flying.

"The main house is being used by the German consul," Mrs. Fauld explained as I helped her out of the taxi. "Dr. Tashian lives in back."

She took my hands and looked at my fingernails. Then she straightened my collar and combed my hair off my forehead.

"You look very handsome," she said. "I'm sure the doctor will be pleased."

I hoped she was right, but I didn't feel very handsome, and I wished that it were two hours from now so that it would all be over and I could breathe normally again. This was the opportunity I had been waiting for, and I was afraid that my nervousness would make me careless or stupid or too quiet or too talkative and that very soon I would be on my way back to the orphanage in another cab.

We walked down a dirt path to the front door of a small stone house, its brown, thatched roof and overhanging eaves making it look like something from a fairy tale. Mrs. Fauld straightened my collar once again, then knocked on the door. It seemed to me that the last two years of my life had been spent standing in front of closed doors, hoping I would be allowed inside. I stood a little on my tiptoes to make myself look taller and expanded my chest to make myself look stronger. A moment later, the door was opened by a short, serious-looking man with black hair, round glasses, and a black suit. He greeted Mrs. Fauld with funereal dignity, then looked at me.

"Dr. Tashian, this is Vahan Kenderian, the boy I told you about."

The doctor nodded and extended his small hand. I

shook it firmly, perhaps a little too firmly, and realized that my hand was wet with perspiration. I had also forgotten to smile.

"Please come in," the doctor said, in a way that convinced me that I was off to a very bad start.

I followed Mrs. Fauld into the house, feeling like the wrong boy, the boy he wasn't expecting, the boy he didn't want. I should have been seventeen or eighteen years old; I should have been Diran or Sisak.

"This is Mrs. Tashian," the doctor said, motioning toward a thin, brown-haired woman whose bright dress offset the somber presence of her husband. Taken separately, the features of her face were unremarkable. Her nose, eyes, and mouth might have belonged to anyone. But the overall sympathy of her features, the warmth of her smile, the understanding in her eyes, made me feel as though I had known her all my life. I shook her hand, and it, too, felt warm and familiar.

By the time I sat down on the couch and Mrs. Tashian offered me tea and pastries, I knew that I had found the home I had been looking for.

I sat on the edge of the couch and tried to look confident and winning. "You have a beautiful house," I said to no one in particular.

Mrs. Tashian thanked me, her eyes shining as though I had said something wonderfully clever.

"I'm sorry we weren't able to welcome you in our own home," the doctor said. "But for now it is the property of the German consul." He put down his tea cup. "You come from Bitlis?"

"Yes," I said.

The doctor spoke a little about Bitlis, then about the war, which he believed would soon be over.

I listened attentively, or, rather, I looked as though I were listening attentively. Actually, I was too nervous to hear a word he said. I was looking for some sign that he liked me, but it was impossible to tell.

"Your father was a lawyer?"

"Yes, sir," I said.

"My wife's father was also a lawyer. In Kars."

I nodded, not knowing whether I was expected to talk about my experiences in Kars or remain silent. My collar felt tight, and I could feel a cold sweat collecting under my arms. I sensed that my chance was slipping away, that the doctor had already decided that I was not the boy he wanted. I looked at Mrs. Fauld, wondering why she didn't say something on my behalf, anything to change the doctor's mind about me. But she was listening politely to whatever he was saying, her hands on her lap. Maybe she already knew it was a lost cause; maybe she had already given up.

"You've been with Mrs. Fauld for three months?"

"Yes. Yes, sir."

Dr. Tashian nodded and swallowed the last of his tea. He put his cup down and looked at me. "You seem like an excellent young man," he said, "but I'm afraid you may be too small for the kind of work you'll have to do here." He turned to Mrs. Fauld. "We need someone a bit older, I think."

I had had enough. "Don't look at my size," I heard myself say, a little louder and more firmly than I intended. "I can do any kind of work you want me to do, and I can work as long as you want me to work. I am very strong, Dr. Tashian. I can harness a wagon and drive it into town and take care of your cow and your horses. I am fourteen years old, but I'm not a boy, and I've been through things harder than this, harder than any work you have for me."

For the first time I met his eyes. "I can do it," I said. "I know I can. Just give me a chance."

No one spoke for a moment. Dr. Tashian looked at Mrs. Fauld, then at his wife.

I was given a small room in the cellar. I cleaned the floor and walls of the room and made my bed with the sheets and comforter I had been given. After dinner, when I returned to my room, there was a vase of flowers on the table beside my bed.

The next morning, Dr. Tashian and I drove the wagon into town and bought supplies for the house. Dr. Tashian offered to help me carry the wood and coal into the storage shed, but I would not let him. I wanted him to see how strong I was and how useful I could be. Later that day, I cleaned the kitchen floor and the shelves where the cups and bowls were kept. I had watched my own servants do this kind of work for many years. At the time, I had thought that there would always be servants for me, and horses to ride, and huge rooms to play in, and crystal glasses to drink from. I had thought that servants were born servants and that they were different from me. Now I knew that they were no different at all.

That night, I lay in my bed, my eyes open. I had fought for myself and won, and now this room was my room. The bed was narrow and the mattress was thin, but it was my bed, my mattress. I had earned them. I had fought for them. I closed my eyes and imagined that my father was smiling. I could feel my father smiling inside me, feel the strength and largeness of my father's presence in my bones.

As the days passed I began to feel less like a servant and more like a son. The chores I did were the chores any child would do for his mother and father, and there was always time to read the books that Mrs.

Tashian gave me or to ride one of the doctor's horses or walk in the hills behind the house. Mrs. Tashian had bought a phonograph in Paris, so there was often music in the house, opera, classical music, French ballads, military marches, and waltzes. She was especially fond of waltzes and would sometimes dance alone, gaily, with no hint of self-consciousness. It was her presence that animated the house, made it seem warm and hospitable.

Every evening she and I talked while she prepared dinner or stored the fruits and vegetables in jars. I told her about my family, and the walks I used to take in the mountains, and the tricks that my friends and I had played on our teachers. I even told her a joke that Uncle Mumpreh had once told me, and she pretended to enjoy it as much as I did. It did not take me long to love her. And with my love came the fear that she would die.

She was plagued by crippling headaches and sometimes stayed in her room all day. They began when she rubbed her eyes, and grew in intensity until her eyes were slits and she could barely see. I brought tea and bread and soup into the dark room where she lay and set the tray beside her, certain that she was dying. I did my chores and worried that any moment the doctor would call me into the house to tell me that she was dead. I prayed for her recovery, and when at last she emerged from her room, it felt as though the house itself had been healed.

With the doctor, I was generally silent and respectful. If the horses were not eating enough, I told the doctor. If a merchant demanded more money for grain or coal, I told the doctor. If the wheel of the wagon needed fixing, the doctor and I would fix it, and he would say "Well done," and that would be that. He seemed to measure out his words and actions with a very small spoon, as though they were precious medicine to be administered in precise doses, and I never once heard him laugh or raise his voice to express either pleasure or anger.

Every two or three days he was summoned to the consulate, where he served as the German consul's personal physician. If it was demoralizing to work in a house that had once been his home, he showed no sign of it, and I am sure he performed his duties stolidly and professionally. In the evenings, however, when Mrs. Tashian asked him about his day, he would say only that he had been to the consulate, and Mrs. Tashian would nod, sympathetically, as if he had complained of some chronic physical ailment, and the subject was dropped. Neither he nor Mrs. Tashian ever mentioned the consul; it was understood that in our house he was a dirty word. And if he was their enemy, he was my enemy, too.

Now and then, when I was working outside, I would glance across the grass field at the consulate, hoping to catch a glimpse of the detested man himself, but I never saw him. One day, however, I did see a girl watching me through one of the two second-story windows. From a distance of seventy yards I could not tell if she was looking at me or another part of the field or nothing at all. I could see only the oval of her face and her brown hair partially lit by the sun.

Being fourteen years old and having nothing to occupy my mind but the weeds I was uprooting in the vegetable garden, I was grateful for any diversion. And so I waved to her, hoping she would wave back. But she didn't. She turned from the window and walked away. Resignedly, I returned to my work, thinking I had seen the last of her.

Chapter Twenty-seven

I was returning from town with a wagon full of supplies when I saw a man striding down the front steps of the consulate toward a waiting black automobile. He was youthful looking, with graying blond hair, a ruddy, overfed face, a small red mouth, and the self-importance of a sultan. I knew immediately that this was the German consul, and I also knew why the doctor and Mrs. Tashian did not like him. He was, at first sight, exceedingly dislikable.

The young woman trailing four or five steps behind him wore a grave, contemplative expression, as though she was on her way to a funeral. She had long brown hair that reached halfway down her back, and she was one of the most beautiful girls or women I had ever seen. If she was his wife, it was certainly an unhappy marriage, and if she was his daughter, she looked ready to run away from home.

As I passed her, she looked at me and raised her right hand slightly, in a kind of secret greeting. She was waving to me, or, rather, waving back, for I recognized her then as the same girl I had seen in the window a few days before. She followed the consul into the waiting automobile and closed the door.

The next time I saw her, I was exercising one of Dr. Tashian's horses and she was standing alone at the far end of the field that separated the consulate from the guest house. There was no question now that it was me she was watching, and without thinking or caring whether she was the consul's wife, secretary, or daughter, I rode toward her, not knowing what I would say when I reached her, or even what language I would say it in.

I was galloping a little faster than usual, hoping to impress her with my skill as a horseman. When I was a few feet from her, I pulled back on the reins with something like panache, and brought the horse around so that I was facing her.

"Hello," I said, anticlimactically, I suppose.

"Hello."

I had forgotten how pretty she was. She was so pretty that, for a moment, I could not think of anything to say. There was a hint of a challenge in her eyes or her smile, as though she was wondering whether or not I would prove myself to be a fool, which, coincidentally, was exactly what *I* was wondering.

"My name is Vahan."

"My name is Seta," she said, and in Armenian added, "Why are you speaking Turkish?"

"You're Armenian?"

"Of course," she said.

She was completely unlike the grave young woman I had seen a few days before. In fact, she looked much more like a girl than a woman, no more than fourteen or fifteen years old. Her face was open now, and friendly, the eyes warm and intelligent. I had the feeling that she was happy to see me, that she had wanted me to come to her.

"Where are you from?"

"Bitlis."

"Bitlis," she said, as though it were the name of a forgotten friend from her past. "It's to the east, in the mountains."

"Yes," I said.

We were both smiling, though neither of us had said anything particularly amusing or even interesting. I was unreasonably, inexplicably happy.

She told me that she came from Erzerum. She had been in Sivas for eight months, and she lived with the German consul.

"Are you his secretary?"

"No." She lowered her eyes a fraction. "I'm his— his guest." She smiled again. "Why did you think I was Turkish?"

"I saw you with the consul, so I assumed you were either German or Turkish, and I didn't speak German."

She nodded at the reasonableness of my logic. Apparently, she had decided that I wasn't a fool.

"I thought you might be his wife," I admitted.

"I'm not his wife," she said. "I just live there. And you live with Dr. Tashian." She pointed across the field at the little house.

"Do you know him?"

"He comes to the consulate almost every day. But he doesn't talk to anyone unless they're sick, and I haven't been sick yet. Werner thinks he's sick every day. He's like an old woman with his complaints."

"Werner?"

"The consul," she said, again lowering her eyes a fraction.

"Is he as vain as he looks?"

She laughed. "More," she said. "He thinks God made the stars to look at him. He stands in front of his mirror gazing at himself like a woman." She imitated the consul looking at himself in the mirror. She made her mouth small and disdainful. "What is your last name, Vahan?"

"Kenderian."

"Vahan Kenderian." She smiled, a ravishing smile. "My name is Seta Boyajian." She extended her hand

and I shook it. I could not help wondering what an Armenian girl was doing in a German consulate. I assumed that the consul had been a friend of her father or mother and was protecting her the way Selim Bey had protected me. It was odd, however, to think of this proud, self-possessed girl needing anyone's protection.

We talked a little longer (all the time knowing that we were going to be friends, that somehow we were already friends), and when it was time to say good-bye and I walked away, I felt strangely as though I was leaving a part of myself behind.

The next day I did my indoor chores as quickly as I could, went outside, sat in the field, and waited for Seta. Though I had only known her for one day, I already missed her and was a little afraid of losing her. I did not think about whether my feelings for her were friendly or romantic. All I knew was that I liked her very much and that if I did not see her that day, I would be unreasonably disappointed.

I looked up at the window where I had first seen her, but she was not there. I was tempted to saunter casually past the front door of the consulate in search of her, but, having more than my own share of pride, I decided against it. I would stay where I was. If she wanted to see me, *she* could saunter casually to the field.

It occurred to me then that we had made no plans to meet and that I had no rational reason to expect her to know that I was waiting for her. Still, I did expect her to know; I expected her to be as impatient to see me as I was to see her. And if she wasn't, then I did not ever want to see her again.

I started to count. When I reached three hundred, I stood up. She wasn't coming.

I sat down again.

Three hundred one, three hundred two . . . Really she was not so special, just an ordinary girl who happened to be Armenian and very pretty. If I did not see her again it would be no real loss—three hundred three, three hundred four . . .

Yes, it would.

Again, I looked up at the second-story window, and again she was not there. She was nowhere in sight. She wasn't coming. There had been no understanding. There had been no friendship. I had imagined it all. Ten minutes passed and I told myself it was foolish to wait any longer.

But I waited anyway.

And a half hour later, my patience was rewarded by the sight of her walking toward me across the field.

My heart soared.

Chapter Twenty-eight

I saw Seta almost every day for the next two months. She was a companion I might have created in my dreams. I felt that I knew her as well as I knew myself, that we had both been alone in empty rooms, had both died and survived in the same way. Hours turned to minutes when I was with her, and every day when we had to leave each other, it always seemed too soon. For a time I told myself that she was nothing more than a friend, but that was not the truth. I thought about her in ways one does not think about a friend, and every time I saw her she seemed more beautiful to me than the time before.

Sometimes, while she was talking, I would think about kissing her and not hear a word she said.

"Where are you?" she would ask.

"Here."

"No, you weren't. What were you thinking?"

"Nothing."

"Be honest, Vahan."

"Nothing."

"Were you thinking, 'I wish that girl would stop talking'?"

"I'm thinking that now."

She smiled. "You won't tell me?"

"It's a secret."

"Do you want me to leave so you can think in private?"

"Yes," I said.

"Then I'm staying. Please tell me."

"No."

"If you won't tell me, then it has to be something important."

"I was thinking that you're pretty."

"No, you weren't."

"I was."

"You think you can cloud my mind with flattery."

I called her a nag, and she laughed. "What were you really thinking?"

"I was thinking that you're my best friend," I said. I had not planned to say that.

Her face softened then, and she looked as though she had just been kissed.

"I'll be your best friend for now," she said, "but if you ever want a new best friend, I'll understand."

"How long have we been talking?"

212

"I don't know," she said. "Do you have to go?"

"I have to sweep out the stable."

"Now?"

I nodded. Then I kissed her on the cheek, the softest cheek I had ever kissed.

"I'll see you tomorrow," I said.

Sometimes when she came to the field she hardly said a word, and there was a quality of melancholy or despair that hovered about her like a fog. "I just feel sad today," she would say, but I knew that it was more than that, that there was a part of her life that she could not share with me, some secret she held closer to herself than our friendship.

She told me once about the consulate, where she had her own room and ate all her meals alone. She told me about the consul, whom she despised:

"At night I hear him in his bedroom. I hear him sniffing when he has a cold. I hear him clear his throat and gargle; I hear him talking to himself; I hear the floor creak beneath his feet. And every sound makes me hate him more, until I hate him so much I can't sleep." She sighed. "If I had a gun I think I would kill him."

I probably smiled at that remark, thinking it a humorous solution to a few minor annoyances. For some reason, I never really asked myself why she hated the consul. Maybe because I was afraid of the answer. It was much easier for me to suppose that she merely disapproved of him, of his arrogance, of the little sounds he made before he went to bed. But I did not believe she really hated him. How could she hate such a silly man?

She tried to tell me once, in her own way:

"There's no luck for Armenians," she said one day. "There's no luck for us at all. Even the survivors are unlucky. Instead of dying once, we have to die every night."

Most Armenian women were round and soft by the time they were fifteen, but Seta's body was still boyish, long, narrow in the hips, and undeveloped in the chest.

As the months passed, however, she began to mysteriously blossom, to grow perceptibly rounder and softer. I told her, half jokingly, that she was becoming a woman, but she insisted that she was just getting fat. "The same thing happened to my mother," she said. And I thought no more about it.

She began to wear loose dresses, but even they could not hide the curious roundness of her belly. I did not realize that she was pregnant until one day when I saw her walking toward me across the field. I had seen women walk that way in Bitlis, proud and smiling, but Seta was not smiling. I knew then that it had never been just she and I, that the consul had been with us all along, and I hated him then, more than I had ever hated anyone in my life. I started to say something and stopped myself. I knew her well enough to know that she would not want me to say a word.

We talked for a few minutes in a slightly strained and artificial way, and then she left. She did not come to see me the next day, or the day after that.

Three days passed and I did not see her. A week passed. I walked to the front of the consulate, but she was not there. I looked through the side windows but did not see her. Every day I looked up from my chores, hoping to see her walking toward me. At night I worried that she was sick or that she had given birth and died.

The doctor still visited the consulate regularly, but he never mentioned Seta. One evening, after dinner, when he and I were alone in the living room, I summoned all my courage and asked him if he had seen her. It was the first time I had ever spoken to him before he spoke to me, and he looked up from his book with mild surprise.

"Who is Seta?"

"The girl who lives in the consulate."

"Is she a friend of yours?"

"Yes," I said.

"I haven't seen her," he said.

And that was that.

I had never known how a heart could break or be sick in just this way, and now, for the first time in my life, I felt an actual break in my heart, a longing that was an actual ache and a sickness. At night I went outside to the field and stared at the window where I first saw her; I stood under that window, waiting for her to appear, willing her to appear. I knew that I loved her, and my heart seemed suddenly strong enough to turn on the light in her room, loud enough to call her to her window. But she never came.

Just before I fell asleep at night, I would imagine I was looking up at her window, where a lamp still burned. Fearlessly, with unimaginable agility, I would scale the wall, open her window, steal silently to her bed, wake her, and carry her to freedom. There would be gunfire, of course, and I would be shot in the leg or the chest, but I would still manage to save her, and once we were outside, beyond the reach of the consul, I would either smile, kiss her, and expire in her arms, or smile, kiss her, collapse to the ground, and expire in her arms. Either way, she cried.

I would imagine a windy night, and in my room I would hear the horses kicking at the walls of their stalls. Running outside, the wind whistling past me, I would look up and see a full moon. The air would smell of some mysterious and intoxicating flower, and high white clouds would be sailing across the sky. The stable doors would be closed, and when I opened them I would find her waiting for me. "I missed you," she would say, and as I embraced her, she would promise never to leave me again.

These were the dreams that filled my days and nights, and late one afternoon, when I had given up hope of ever seeing her again, they came true: I was walking out of the stable when I saw her sitting on the front steps of the house. It was really her this time, and though I knew immediately that there would be no kiss or proclamation of love, I was every bit as elated to see her as I had been on that imaginary windy night.

"Hello, Vahan."

Her stomach was bigger now, but, at first glance, she looked the same. I sat beside her, and it was as though no time had been lost, as though we had been sitting beside each other all along.

"He threw me out," she said very calmly.

"The consul?"

"He didn't want this," she said, touching her stomach. She sounded very calm, her voice uninflected, as if she were talking in her sleep.

217

"When?"

"Today. This morning. He said it was disgusting. That's what he said in German. 'Disgusting.' He said I was too fat and he couldn't . . ." She did not say it, but I understood. "I started to walk into town, and then I came here. I didn't know what else to do." She looked at me then, beseechingly, the way I must have looked at Mrs. Altoonian when I went to her door after begging on the street.

And I did not know what to say. In none of my dreams did it matter that I was not Dr. and Mrs. Tashian's son and had no right to bring Seta into their house without telling them. In none of my dreams was there a Dr. Tashian telling me that there was no room and no food for Seta and that she would have to leave. Yet here was Seta, with nowhere to go, and I could not take the chance that Dr. Tashian would not let her stay. I had no other choice.

"Come with me," I said, helping her to her feet. I opened the front door soundlessly and looked inside. The living room was empty, and I heard Mrs. Tashian in the kitchen. I grabbed Seta's hand, and we crossed the living room as quickly and quietly as we could. I opened the door that led to the basement and walked her carefully down the stone steps to my room.

She sat down on the bed. Her face was drawn, and

she looked small despite the size of her belly. I asked her if she was hungry, and she shook her head. She suddenly seemed helpless.

"You have to eat," I said.

She nodded. And then she covered her face with her hands and she was crying. I put my arm around her and her body shook; her body was shaking and her hands were hiding her face. She turned toward me and I put my arms around her, and her head was buried in my chest and she was shaking in my arms. I had no handkerchief to give her, so I gave her one of my shirts, and she wiped her nose and eyes.

"I'm sorry I didn't tell you," she said. "I was too ashamed."

"It's his shame, not yours," I said.

"I should have run away."

"Where would you go?"

She didn't answer.

"There was nowhere to go," I said.

That night I ate my dinner in silence, the secret I carried growing heavier by the second. Mrs. Tashian asked me if I was all right, and I said I was fine. I felt as though I was betraying her trust; I felt like a bad son. Tomorrow, I would tell Dr. Tashian everything, and if he would not let Seta stay, I would go away with her.

After dinner, I took her some food I had smuggled from the kitchen, sat in the chair by the bed, and watched her eat.

"Are you tired?" I said, instead of "I love you."

She nodded.

"You should go to sleep."

She shook her head. "Am I still your best friend?"

"Yes," I said. She looked very tired. "Go to sleep."

"Do you think Dr. Tashian will let me stay?"

"Yes," I lied.

When she could not keep her eyes open any longer, I turned off the lamp. I sat in the chair and watched her sleep. It no longer mattered what had brought her here. All that mattered was that we were together, that she did not have to go anywhere alone tonight or ever again.

Early the next morning, I ran my fingers through my hair and started up the stairs to talk to Dr. Tashian. I had spent most of the night thinking about what I would say, and now all the separate lines of the story had become knotted in my mind. "I have a friend . . ." I would begin, and then I would tell him that Seta was pregnant, that the consul had thrown her out of the house, that she had no family, and that she had nowhere to go. She could sleep in my bed, and I would sleep in the chair. I would give her half my food and take care of her until it was time for the baby to come.

I was sure that Dr. Tashian would understand. But then it did not seem enough to say that she was pregnant and had nowhere to go. It did not seem enough that I was the only friend she had.

I closed the basement door behind me, wondering what more I could say.

"Good morning, Vahan."

It was Mrs. Tashian.

I said good morning.

I said I had slept well.

Yes, I was ready for breakfast. But I had something to tell her.

"I have a friend . . ." I began.

Seta had been sleeping when I left the room, but now she was standing by the bed, her hair pulled back, her face so pale that I thought that she was going to faint. When she saw Mrs. Tashian, she crossed her arms in front of her to hide her stomach. Mrs. Tashian smiled and kissed her cheek and said that she was very happy to meet Vahan's friend. She did not mention the consul, and she did not mention the baby.

"The doctor and I would be very happy if you would stay with us," she said.

Chapter Twenty-nine

Despite Mrs. Tashian's objections, Seta insisted on making herself useful. She dusted the furniture, helped wash the clothes, and even made bread in the toneer. Like me, she had not had a family in two years, and now, free from the consul, from the consulate, from loneliness and solitude, she began to flourish. As the light will illuminate each colored chip of a kaleidoscope, so Seta's happiness began to illuminate every aspect of her being, every gesture, every word, the sound of her voice, the tilt of her head, and the way she sat. I could see her happiness even when her back was turned to me, and having her in my life was an answer to many prayers.

Mrs. Tashian knitted a white blanket for the baby, and Dr. Tashian and I made a cradle from the wood we bought in town. (Actually, Dr. Tashian made the cradle by himself, and I watched him and pretended I was learning something.) Every evening, prayers were said for the health and good fortune of the baby, and every morning Mrs. Tashian lit a white candle and placed it on the table beside the couch where Seta slept.

Personally, I did not understand what all the fuss was about. As far as I was concerned, the child was nothing more than a bulge in her stomach, a dividing line whose birth would allow me to transform my silent love for Seta into a spoken one. Until then I would be the friend she needed me to be and keep my heart a secret.

She told me one night that she was going to name the baby Krikor, after her father.

"How do you know it's going to be a boy?"

"My mother knew I was going to be a girl, and this baby is going to be a boy." Just then she looked at her stomach and held it with both hands. "Oh, Vahan, he's kicking. Do you want to feel him?"

I did not answer. I had never touched a pregnant woman's stomach before, and I did not want to start now. Seta took my hand and placed it on her belly.

"I want him to know my best friend," she said.

A moment later, I felt the skin move under my fingers, and my hand jumped and she laughed and put it back and I felt another kick.

"Did you feel that?"

I nodded, amazed, staring at my hand. He had not been real to me, and now, somehow, he was as real as

Seta herself. I felt the baby move once again, and, involuntarily, my heart seemed to open and I could suddenly see the family he would make of us.

"I'm going to be a mother, Vahan," Seta said, smiling.

When her pains began, Dr. and Mrs. Tashian took her into their bedroom with hot water and blankets and sheets and strips of cloth. I stood outside the closed door, waiting, listening.

Dr. Tashian had warned me that it might be a difficult birth. "She's too narrow here," he said, touching his hips. "She should be a little older."

But I knew better. I knew that it would be a swift and painless delivery and that it was only a matter of seconds before Mrs. Tashian opened the door and invited me into the bedroom to celebrate our new life.

I heard Seta moaning, asking the doctor if he could stop the pain. Two hours passed, and I was pacing from the doctor's chair in the living room to the closed door of the bedroom. Seven hours later it was the same, only Seta's pain was worse. She cried for it to stop, to stop, to please stop, to please stop it. I listened at the door, waiting for the pain to end.

"Is he going to come?"

"Yes, he's going to come, Seta."

"Yes?"

"Yes. I promise."

"Why hasn't he come?"

"He will."

"He won't." She began to cry.

"He'll come, Seta," Mrs. Tashian's voice gently assured her.

In Bitlis, babies seemed to simply appear. A woman was pregnant, several months passed, the moment arrived, and the next day there was a baby. No one said anything about screaming for hours and begging God to stop the pain. And even if it was normal for women to suffer pain, I was certain that this kind of pain was not normal.

I smelled the burning incense through the door and heard Mrs. Tashian say:

". . . light of Christ.

". . . breath of our Savior.

". . . give you comfort and strength."

Sometime in the early hours of the following day, Seta's screams became groans, panting and rhythmical, and below them the doctor's voice, a monotone, telling her to push, and push again, and push harder, harder.

"Is he coming?"

"He's coming. Keep pushing."

"Is he coming?"

"He's coming, Seta. Push."

And the cry of her effort, of an animal, of exhaustion. And silence.

I said a prayer and crossed myself. And then the door opened, and Mrs. Tashian, very pale, told me it was a boy.

I was allowed to see Seta later that day. The afternoon sunlight slanted into the room through half-closed shutters, and the room still smelled of the incense that had purified it the night before. She was sitting up in bed, cradling her son in her arms. When she saw me, she smiled, and my heart swelled, and for some reason I felt like crying. I sat on the edge of the bed, kissed her on the cheek, and looked at the sleeping baby. I tried to see Seta in his face, but I couldn't. All I saw was a shriveled old man. I had never seen a newborn infant before, so I assumed that he would grow up to be as ugly as he was at that moment. I looked at Seta pityingly. "How do you feel?"

She pulled the blanket down to her waist and touched her stomach. "I'm not fat," she said.

Her voice was weak, but I guessed that that was normal. She looked tired, and her face was pale, but I guessed that that was normal, too.

"Do you want to sleep?"

"Not now," she said. "He's ugly, isn't he?"

"He's not ugly, Seta."

"He is. He's the ugliest baby I've ever seen."

"Maybe that's how he's supposed to look."

"Did you see his head? He has a head like an eggplant."

I started to laugh, and Seta put her finger to her lips so I wouldn't wake the baby. "You heard me? Last night?"

I nodded.

"Poor Vahan," she said with a smile. Her voice seemed to be getting weaker.

"You need to rest," I said, and kissed her cheek. Then, because she was alive, because I had been so afraid I would lose her, I kissed her once more.

As I closed the bedroom door behind me, this is how I envisioned the next ten years of my life:

I saw a family raising a child, growing happier every day. I saw Krikor take his first steps, heard him speak his first words. I saw Seta and me talking together in the field, working together in the garden. I saw myself take her hand at last, kiss her lips at last, tell her at last what was in my heart. I saw myself grown, a lawyer now, and Mrs. Tashian as proud as my own mother would have been, and Dr. Tashian clasping my hand and looking into my eyes with a father's love and pride.

I saw Seta at my side, her hand in mine. And now our own children, a home of our own, and Krikor grown and handsome and healthy.

This was the life I imagined, and I closed my hand and held it.

But only for a night.

The next morning, Seta had a fever. She asked for glass after glass of water. It seemed that she could not drink enough water. "She needs to rest and regain her strength," Dr. Tashian told me. But looking at him, at the expression on his face, I suspected that he was not telling me all he knew, or feared.

The next day, Seta was weaker, and now she could not sit up in bed without help, and it seemed as though all the light and color had gone from her face. I sat by her bed and read to her because her vision was blurred and she could not see the words clearly. Mrs. Tashian gave her bread and soup, but she had no appetite and could only eat a few bites. All she wanted was water. After examining her, Dr. Tashian told Mrs. Tashian and me to come into the kitchen. I knew before we got there; I didn't want to know, but I knew.

She had an infection, he said, caused by an internal rupture sustained during delivery. The poison from the infection was polluting her bloodstream. "She was not big enough to deliver a baby of that size."

"Is she going to die?"

He did not answer at first. "There's nothing I can do to help her," he said.

She was going to die. I saw it very clearly. And the next moment I knew that she wouldn't. A rupture was just a kind of cut, I told myself, and cuts healed. She *could* die, but she wouldn't. I felt very strongly that she wouldn't die.

When I went back to her room, she asked for water, and I gave it to her. I felt her forehead, walked calmly out of the room, then ran to the doctor.

Over the next three days her fever climbed. Her lips were cracked and dry, and her vision grew worse. The doctor listened to her heart and looked in her eyes; he felt her forehead and looked in her mouth, but there was nothing he could give her, nothing he could do. Mrs. Tashian prayed by her bed. I prayed in my own room. I asked God not to let her die. I asked God to make her strong again. But I knew she was going to die, and I cried as though she were already dead.

She lost consciousness on the fifth day of her illness. I sat beside her and watched her gray face. I held her hand and kissed her fingers and loved her so much that my heart ached. I saw then that the dying have before them a window through which no one can pass. Though I was close enough to hear her breathe, close enough to take her hand and caress and kiss her cheek, I could not get close enough to save her life. I could only watch it slip away.

Seven days after she had given birth, she was dead. Dr. Tashian and I wrapped her in a blanket and buried her in the field. Two men from the consulate watched us dig the grave. The next day, one of them came to the house and told Dr. Tashian that the consul wanted the baby. Dr. and Mrs. Tashian begged the consul to let them keep him, but the consul refused. Later, we heard he had sent the baby to his sisters in Germany.

Chapter Thirty

The house seemed empty for many weeks. Chores were done, meals were eaten, conversations begun and ended without anything having really been said. I tried to close my mind to Seta and be who I had been before I knew her. I told myself that nothing had really changed. Only Seta was gone, and, except for the lavosh bread that she had made and stored, there was no evidence that she had existed at all. If I was a little more irritable than usual, if the cow did not seem to give milk fast enough, or my bed suddenly seemed too small, or the squeaking of a certain door suddenly seemed intolerable and I found myself hitting the door with the heel of my hand, well, that had nothing to do with Seta.

Sometimes, however, when I was working alone in the garden, I would know that she was not helping Mrs. Tashian in the kitchen, not resting on the couch, or on her way outside to see me; I would know then that she was really gone and that some essential shade of color or quality of light had left the sky.

One night I tried to talk to Mrs. Tashian about it, but I did not know what to say. "I miss her," I said, several times, but it was not enough, it was nothing, only a phrase standing like a soldier over a feeling I could not describe. She kissed me, and I saw my own pain in her eyes. She turned out the lamp, and I wanted to say more, but I had no words.

"Good night," I said.

I realize now that I had been thinking only of myself. I had not noticed the toll the last several weeks had taken on Mrs. Tashian. I thought that I was the only one who could miss Seta, who had seen a family and a future in her baby, who had loved her and cried for her. It was impossible to see all the wear behind Mrs. Tashian's familiar face, to hear it behind her lovely voice.

Three days later, she had a stroke, and two days after that she was dead.

Dr. Tashian and I buried her near the garden. Dr. Tashian said a prayer. Our heads were bowed, and I listened to his calm, paternal voice administer the prayer as he might any other medication—competently and without emotion. And then, abruptly, his voice began to falter and he stopped. He tried again to speak, and again he stopped. I looked at him then, at his darkened profile and small, somber frame. We were standing only a few feet from each other, yet I felt we were both alone, with only our sorrow in common. I wanted to say or do something to console him, but even then he was not a man you could touch.

There were only the two of us now in a house of empty rooms, of walls and windows. The house was kept dark for one week, and we said only the things that we had to say to each other: "Good morning" and "Good night" and a few words in between. I tried to make his life as comfortable as possible, but everything had ended, and the house was no longer my home. It was only a place where Seta and Mrs. Tashian no longer lived, a museum of the things that had once been theirs: the unwound clock, the empty chair, the unlit candle. . . .

I did not want to stay in Sivas anymore. I hated Sivas now.

Chapter Thirty-one

The autumn of 1917 came with rain and wind and fog that seemed to erase the world. Gasoline was scarce, and German trucks and automobiles were abandoned on the streets of Gavra and on the road that led to the consulate. Mules and horses and wagons had to be bought to move German supplies north to Samsun. From Samsun it was only four days by boat to Constantinople, where it was rumored that the Armenian population was safe. With Seta and Mrs. Tashian gone, I was now as thirsty and hungry for that kind of freedom as I had been for food and water on the march to the river. Without them, all I had in the world was the promise of that freedom, and I would rather die a young man trying to find it than survive a hundred more years hiding in the homes and stables of Sivas or Bitlis or Kars.

I stood in a line of would-be wagon drivers, nervously waiting for my turn. In preparation for this moment, I had stolen a Turkish army uniform from one of several boxes outside the army barracks a mile from the town. It was a poor fit, but with the sleeves and trouser legs folded inside and pinned, I looked presentable. I stood as straight as a soldier, my arms stiff at my sides, my chest thrust forward. A German officer, followed closely by an Armenian interpreter, was interviewing each man in the line.

"What is your name?" the officer asked me through the translator.

"Vahan Kenderian."

"Armenian?"

"Yes," I said.

The German officer looked at me with something like distaste. "How old are you?"

The question was translated.

"Eighteen," I lied.

The interpreter smiled slightly. "Eighteen years old," he said to the German officer. The officer squeezed my shoulders and upper arms. "You know how to drive a wagon?"

The Armenian translated the question.

"Yes," I said.

The interpreter said something to the officer and turned to me. In Armenian he said, "I told him that I have seen you drive a wagon of three horses. How old are you really?"

I did not answer.

"Eighteen is better," the interpreter said. "Say something to me."

"What do you want me to say?"

"That's fine." He said something to the officer, and the officer nodded. The interpreter turned to me. "I told him that you said you are a loyal citizen of the empire."

"Three horses," the officer said.

"Three horses," the interpreter said to me. "You leave in the morning."

I waited until the evening to tell Dr. Tashian that I was going. He did not seem surprised. He nodded, showing no sign of whether he was happy or sorry to see me go, gave me his blessing, and we shook hands. I should have embraced him. I should have clasped his hand with my two hands and thanked him for giving me a home, for taking care of Seta and trying to keep her baby. But I didn't. Maybe because at that moment all I saw before me was a man I hardly knew, a man I respected but did not love.

"For your new life," he said, handing me two ten-lira notes.

I started to thank him, but he shook his head. "It comes from Mrs. Tashian," he said. "She would never forgive me if I did not give you something."

I left early the next morning, before the doctor was awake. I tiptoed across the living-room floor, past a hundred memories, closed the front door behind me, and started through the early-morning fog and drizzle toward the consulate, where I had been told to report.

On the road in front of the consulate was a line of five wagons, each with a team of three horses. Near the gates stood five German soldiers, some conversing in their mysterious language, some glancing impatiently at the two Turkish civilians who were loading the wagons with boxes. The newly hired drivers, all Turkish, were standing here and there, looking grim and solitary in the early morning. It did not seem to matter to them where they were going or how long it would take to get there or whether the sky was blue or gray. They were old horses waiting to be mounted, spurred, and driven, and in their eyes I could see that every day was the same and every road led nowhere.

I stood beside the last wagon, hoping I did not look as young as I felt. I did my best to mimic the general expression of boredom, for I did not want anyone to know how green I really was or how much this day meant to me. Also, if I was really a man at last, I wanted to wear the mask of a man—the knowing gaze, the frown and creases.

Some of the drivers were smoking, and I wished I had a cigarette, too, for seasoning. Impulsively, I walked up to the least threatening-looking driver of the bunch and, in my best Turkish accent, asked him for a cigarette.

"Armenian, eh?" he said.

Before I could answer, he shrugged, reached into his pocket, and handed me a rolled cigarette. I put the cigarette in my mouth and the driver lit it.

"How old are you?"

"Eighteen," I said, narrowing my eyes a little in an attempt to look callous and world-weary.

"You know how to drive three horses?"

I didn't. I had never driven three horses in my life. "Of course," I said.

The driver was not fooled. "It doesn't matter to me," he said. "It's not my wagon. All these Germans can go over a cliff as far as I'm concerned. Which one is yours?"

I pointed to the last wagon.

"I'm just ahead of you," he said. "If you don't know what to do, just watch me. My name is Aziz."

"I'm Vahan," I said.

He handed me another cigarette. "Good fortune," he said.

After all the wagons were loaded, I climbed onto

the last rig, sat on the driver's board beside a German soldier, and took the reins. And now I did not need a cigarette or a mask to feel like a man. I was holding the reins of my own life, looking over the backs of three horses to a destination I had chosen—Constantinople and freedom.

The first wagon began to roll, then the second and the third. I shook the reins. I looked back at the field, at Seta and me, then looked ahead.

For three days I followed the other wagons like a veteran. We passed abandoned villages, orchards of olive trees, and farmers who looked up from ox-drawn plows. The road was straight and level. All I had to do was hold on to the reins, dream of Constantinople, and let the hours pass under my wheels. Now and then Aziz would look back at me to see how I was doing, but I could have told him he had nothing to worry about. Driving three horses was no different from driving one, and as I grew more confident of that fact, I began to look about myself with something like the old arrogance. As the road climbed and the days grew colder, as pale green fields turned gold, then brown, I held fast to the notion that I was the master of my fate.

On the fourth day, we passed Tokat and entered

the mountains. The dirt road was muddy and pooled with water, and the air smelled of wet earth and rain. Beyond the left edge of the road, the mountain dropped thirty, then fifty, then a hundred feet to a rocky valley. As the road climbed, my concern gave way to alarm, alarm to fear, and fear to near panic. I kept my horses as far from the edge of the road as I could, knowing that one mistake on my part or one misstep on theirs and we would all be tumbling down the mountain to our doom. It was a terrifying realization made worse by the fact that the road ahead narrowed and curved sharply to the right. Foolishly, I looked below, and was quickly assured that my death, if I fell, would be instantaneous.

As the drivers approached the curve they stood and reined their horses hard to the right. The space between their left rear wheels and the edge of the road could not have been more than a few inches. I was sitting up straighter now, gripping the reins.

The wagon ahead of mine, Aziz's wagon, was nearing the curve. I watched him stand and pull his reins to the right. I watched his wheels. I watched the way he held the reins; I saw that they were taut, seeming to cut into the sweat-soaked necks of his horses. He looked to be in complete control. And then, with a suddenness that stopped my heart, the left end of his wagon dropped. He had taken the turn wide and his left rear wheel had rolled over the edge. His horses stopped. He shook the reins frantically, but his horses would not move. He whipped and cursed the horses, and the horses backed up and the back half of his wagon disappeared. And then, with a scraping of wood on rock, the wagon slid back over the edge, the front end rising, flipping Aziz and the German beside him backward into the bed of the wagon, and with a final crack as the raised right front wheel caught the rocks at the edge of the road, snapping it from the axle, the wagon toppled down the side of the mountain, dragging the horses after it. I heard the two men scream, and the crash as the wagon hit the rocks below.

I froze. My wagon was approaching the curve, and I pulled back on the reins. The German soldier beside me was on his feet, trying to see into the valley. He waved me forward, but I could not move. The road was too narrow, and beyond its edge I saw my own death.

My horses were backing up now toward the edge of the road, and I did not know whether to drop the reins or shake them or pull them back. *"Fahrweiter, schnell!"* the German said, grabbing the reins and shaking them wildly. *"Fahrweiter, schnell!"* I was paralyzed, staring at the curve in the road a few feet ahead. One of the Turkish drivers took the reins from the German, grabbed my arm, and put the reins in my hand. "Pull them to the right," he said.

I started to refuse, to hand him the reins and jump off the wagon. But something stopped me. I did not want to run to my mother's room this time; I did not want to rely on Sisak to pull me into the river or across the street to hide from the gendarmes. This was my wagon and I had to take it around the turn myself, because if I didn't, I knew I could not survive in Samsun or Constantinople or anywhere else in the world.

I shook the reins and pulled them hard to the right, but the horses would not move. The Turk ran to the front of the wagon and tried to pull the horses forward. "Whip them!" he said.

I picked up the stick.

"Whip them!"

I hit the horses again and again.

"Harder!"

I hit them harder; I hit them as hard as I could. Slowly, the wagon began to move. When it was around the curve, the Turkish driver walked to the edge of the road, looked below, and walked back to his wagon.

In my dreams that night it was my wagon that disappeared, and it was my own screams I heard when I awoke in the dark.

Chapter Thirty-two

We continued on, past Amasia, past Marsovan. As the road descended to Samsun, the air began to smell of the sea, and stands of olive trees appeared on the hills. Through the mist beyond the hills, I saw a patch of the Black Sea—my pathway to freedom and a new life. It disappeared when the road turned and dropped, then appeared again, clearer and wider and more thrilling than before. Excitement to match my own spread from wagon to wagon, and now the German soldiers were calling to one another and pointing in the direction of the sea. A horn blew in the distance, then another. The sea disappeared behind the hills, and when it reappeared, I saw three battleships in the harbor. The ships' horns blew again and again, and now I had to whip my horses to keep up with the wagons ahead. The soldier beside me said something that I did not understand, grabbed the reins, and shook them harder. *"Mach schnell!"* he said. *"Mach schnell!"*

When we were a mile or two from the harbor, the

wagons stopped. Without a word, the soldier beside me jumped down from the wagon and walked quickly in the direction of the battleships. Incredibly, the other Germans followed, leaving their boxes behind on the wagons. When the battleships blew their horns again, the soldiers began to run.

"What are they doing?" I said. But no one answered. When the soldiers were out of sight, the other drivers, as if by prior arrangement, shook their reins and drove away, each in a different direction. It was probably a comical moment, though, being alone in the center of a dirt road on the outskirts of a strange city, I saw nothing funny about it. Also, it was getting dark. I listened, hoping to hear the sounds of a city, but I heard nothing. Thinking that I ought to do something, I shook the reins and drove down one of the roads. After about half a mile, I stopped. It occurred to me that without an entourage of four wagons and the presence of German soldiers, I was only an Armenian, as vulnerable in Samsun as I had been in Bitlis and Andreas and Kars. I had no evidence that I was really a driver for the Turkish army, and I did not want to be accused of stealing a military uniform and wagon, so I stepped down, unharnessed the horses, and started to walk.

Many miles later, the narrow dirt road widened, and in the distance I saw the pale light of a streetlamp and the deserted street it illuminated. On either side of the street were blocks of shadows that in the morning would become the ironsmith's shop, the butcher shop, the general store. I saw several groups of men standing in a dirt field beside their wagons. I saw the open boxes that contained their produce. They were farmers waiting for the morning, for market day. I stood a safe distance from them and listened: The men were speaking a language I had never heard. There was a boy sitting alone on a crate beside one of the wagons. I quickly crossed the twenty-five yards of darkness that separated us and, in a voice intentionally deeper and more threatening than my own, said in Turkish (the safest language one stranger could speak to another), "What language are those men speaking?"

The boy looked up, startled. "Greek," he said.

"You're Greek?" I could not have been more relieved if he had said he was Armenian. The Greeks, aside from being fellow Christians, were fellow victims of the Turks.

"Yes," the boy said.

"I am Armenian."

The boy nodded warily, as though I had told him I was a ghost. I did not realize then how rare Armenians in Turkey had become. Also, I had forgotten I was wearing the uniform of the Turkish army.

"Wait," he said. "Wait here." He ran to a big-bellied man who was with several others who were tossing coins at a spot in the darkness. At that distance, all I could see was his huge mustache. It was as bushy as a sultan's, nearly covering the bottom third of his face. As he followed the boy back to me, he swiped a piece of fruit from the open box of one of the farmers, took a huge bite, then tossed a coin six or seven feet into the box.

"My name is Spiros Koulouris," he said, addressing me in Turkish. He smiled broadly, but his eyes were shrewd, watchful. "You're Armenian?"

"Yes," I said.

"From where?"

"Bitlis."

The man nodded. He was squat and barrel-chested, with thick forearms and a heavy, beard-stubbled face. Despite his suspicions, there was a sense of vitality and well-being about him that seemed to fill the night.

"Why are you wearing a Turkish uniform?" he asked.

"There are many Armenians in the Turkish army," I said. "This belonged to my cousin."

"Your cousin was a soldier?"

"Yes," I said.

"What was his name?"

"If I'm speaking to a friend and not a gendarme, what business is it of yours?"

"It is not my business at all, *if* you're Armenian. But I have helped a few Armenians here and there, so I must be a little careful."

"And how did you know that the others were really Armenians?"

The man did not answer at first. Then he smiled, as though the question of my veracity had just been settled. "From Bitlis," he said. "You're lucky to be alive. What is an Armenian from Bitlis doing in Samsun?"

"I want to go to Constantinople," I said.

"You have money?"

"I have a few lira."

"A *few* lira. You'll need more than a *few* lira. How many lira?"

I started to take off my shoe to show him one of the ten-lira notes (I had taken the precaution of putting one in each shoe), but he held up his hand. "Do you show every stranger where you keep your money?" he said.

"You're not a stranger," I said, foolishly.

"You have known me five minutes and I am not a stranger? I think you make friends too quickly. Everyone you meet is a stranger until he *proves* that he is your friend. Do you have more than seven lira?"

"Yes," I said.

"Then I can help you. What is your name?"

"Vahan Kenderian."

"Vahan. All right, Vahan. Tomorrow you will meet a man who will ask you the same questions I am asking you now. And this man will not care whether or not you know how to hold on to your money. If you tell him how much you have, that is how much he will want. Are you hungry?"

Before I could answer, he turned to his son. "Manolis! Get the boy some bread." To me: "If you have money in your other shoe, take it out and put it somewhere else."

"Now?"

"Not now. When you are sure you are not being watched. You like melon?"

"Yes," I said.

"Get one of the melons," he called to his son. "And the knife. Bring the knife."

That night, I lay in the back of Spiros Koulouris's wagon. Beside me, Manolis slept. Spiros Koulouris was asleep on the driver's board, under a blanket. I listened to him snore for several minutes, then I took off one of my shoes, removed a ten-lira note, rolled it tightly, and put it in my sock. Satisfied, I closed my eyes.

"Good boy," the Greek said in a startlingly clear voice. "Now get some sleep."

When I awoke the next morning, Manolis and his father were gone and the dirt field was crowded with marketers. I sat up and, in the distance, saw Spiros Koulouris talking to a slight man of indeterminate age. He stood very close to Mr. Koulouris, his arms folded, his head cocked, listening. He nodded once, then looked at the wagon where I was sitting.

The two men started toward me, and I stepped down from the wagon and watched them approach.

"I am a friend of Mr. Koulouris," the gray man said to me. He had a gray, middle-aged face, thinning gray hair, and the flat, impersonal eyes of a ticket taker at a carnival. With a glance he reduced my entire history and physical relevance to a hand holding a ticket. "You want to go to Constantinople?"

"Yes."

"Do you have any relatives there?"

"Yes," I lied. "I have many relatives."

"It will cost you money," the man said.

"How much?"

"Can you pay fifteen lira?"

"No," I said. "I don't have that much money."

"You have ten lira?"

"If I give you ten lira, I won't have anything left."

"Show me your money."

I looked at Spiros Koulouris, who nodded once, almost imperceptibly. I took off my shoe and withdrew the ten-lira note.

"That's all you have?"

"Yes."

"Give me eight lira when we board the ship. Two will be enough for you." He said something in Greek to Mr. Koulouris, who laughed.

"What did he say?" I asked.

"He says that if you were not my friend he would ask you to take off your other shoe."

Chapter Thirty-three

Early in the afternoon, Mr. Koulouris's friend drove me in his wagon down the dirt path that led to the harbor, the same path that had led me to Spiros Koulouris the night before.

When we reached the harbor, I followed him along a wood walkway, past a line of deserted slips. My experience with boats being limited to drawings I had seen in books, I assumed that they all had towering masts, billowing sails, and a battalion of oars poised evenly over the surface of an inky sea. Therefore, if I had seen a Roman slave ship or a Spanish galleon at the end of the walkway, I would not have been surprised. What I saw, however, was an ungainly-looking vessel with a squat metal hull and a phalanx of machinery. No oars, no sails, no masts, just one hundred fifty feet of metal swaying sluggishly against an unseen anchor.

We ascended a wood plank and stepped onto a green metal deck. I felt then as though I had stepped onto another world, an alien and self-contained world with its own language, laws, and rules of behavior. A handful of sullen-looking men stood by the rails, some glancing over their shoulders at us as though we were two empty bottles that had just been tossed onto their deck: In a world where every man, every piece of metal, every block of wood had a function, our presence was, at best, superfluous, and, at worst, an insult.

Mr. Koulouris's friend led me down a steep metal stairway, down an airless corridor, to a small, empty room. Actually, it was more like a container, a windowless, green-walled container designed either for the storage of unusable ship parts or the transport of heartsick refugees. There was no bed, no chairs, no sink, and very little air. What air there was, was oppressive and sour smelling and crowded with the presence of past sufferers.

"This is where you will stay," he said. "You don't leave this room. All right?"

"All right," I said.

"Give me your eight lira."

I handed him the ten-lira note, and he gave me two coins.

"I'll be back," he said, closing the door behind him.

I was too excited to sit quietly, so I walked around the little room. I was tempted to go on deck, but I did not want to risk being thrown off the ship for insubordination, so I sat against one of the walls and waited. I knew that I was probably free, but I wouldn't let myself believe it. As far as I was concerned, I still lived in a world where Mr. Koulouris's friend was a fraud who took money from Armenian boys and then had them arrested by the gendarmes. In my mind there would be no true freedom until I reached Constantinople.

An hour later, Mr. Koulouris's friend returned with a boy about my age. He had a sallow, friendly face and black, dirt-streaked hair. The jacket he wore was too big for him, and his trousers were faded, dirt smeared and mud caked.

Mr. Koulouris's friend took the boy's money and told him not to leave the room. He disappeared for a moment and returned with a jar of water, a lamp, a matchbox, and a bag filled with bread. "You will be in Constantinople in four days," he said. "Good luck."

The boy's name was Gagik; he came from Samsun, and, like me, he had never been on a boat before. He seemed reluctant to talk at first, and I guessed he was shy, though, of course, it is hard to draw any definitive conclusions about the native personality of one who has lost his home and his family. I asked him how he knew Mr. Koulouris's friend, and he said he had met him at the harbor. "Did you trust him?" I asked.

"I had to," he said.

Just then the ship's horn sounded. Above us we heard footsteps going up and down the metal stairs. The engines vibrated the walls of our small room, and my heart began to beat a little faster. And then I felt the boat begin to move, and I knew as I had not known before that I was really leaving, that this ship was taking me away from the shore of my country, the shore of my home, the shore of the boy I had been, and the life and the people I had loved. And as the boat drew itself farther out to sea, I longed for that life as I had not longed for it before. I longed for my mother's face and voice; my heart was a scream for my mother sounding over the face of the land I was leaving—for the brown hair she had had, for her bones and her rags.

For the first few hours of the voyage I slept a black sleep. I awoke to find Gagik sleeping a few feet from me. I sat up, lit the lamp, listened to the steady hum of the engines, and felt the long minutes pass. When Gagik awoke, he picked up the bag of bread, opened it, looked inside, then put it down.

"What time do you think it is?" he said.

I shook my head. It did not matter what time it was. Our twenty-four-hour day of sunlight and darkness had been replaced by the ninety-six-hour span of

sea that separated us from Constantinople, a nauseat-
ing eternity of bread and water, lamplight and rolling
waves.

"I wish it was tomorrow," Gagik said.

I nodded listlessly. I was beginning to feel sick in a
way I had never felt sick before. Remembering that I
had not eaten all day, I reached for the bag of bread,
but just the thought of eating made me queasy, so I
closed my eyes and tried to sleep, feeling the rigid bulk
of the ship rise and fall as it inched its way along the
surface of the water.

I turned on my side, so that I faced the wall, and
drew my legs up to my chest. I swallowed, and my
tongue felt fat in my mouth, as though it were someone
else's tongue. Thinking I needed air, I got to my feet
and threw open the door, but the corridor was as hu-
mid and airless as the room. When I sat down, the ship
rocked and the door slammed shut. I lay down on
the floor and began to rock back and forth, moaning
softly, keeping perfect time with the rolling of the ship
on the waves.

Around this time I realized I had been listening to
a second set of moans, similar to my own but in a
slightly different key. I turned and looked at Gagik,
who had slumped a little down the wall, his face pale
and moist in the light.

"What's wrong?" I said.

He shook his head. He started to speak and threw up on his pants.

For three days we were too seasick to eat or drink. The bag of bread lay in a corner where I had thrown it the second night. The jar of water was used as a doorstop. Every day someone would kick the jar over and close the door. "It stinks in there," a voice would say, or nothing was said at all.

When we could talk, we talked about Constantinople, about palaces and bazaars and endless streets of endless possibilities. Gagik had heard that every day was market day, and that all the lights on the streets turned night into day. I said I had heard that every fountain was filled with gold coins, though in fact I had heard no such thing. Our misery worked upon the city like a magician, transforming glass into crystal, brick into gold, the earthly into the ethereal. And the more miserable we were, the more wondrous and fantastical Constantinople became, until finally it seemed more a creation of a genie than of architects and stonecutters.

Worse than the seasickness was the time I spent with my own thoughts. Sometimes it was Diran who stepped forward, sometimes Sisak or Armenouhi. But most often and most painfully, it was Oskina—reading me stories when I was sick, changing my wet sheets late at night when I was four years old, chasing me through the house when I accidentally broke her bracelet, smiling beside me in a photograph. I embraced her by the river and said good-bye a hundred times, knowing I had had no other choice, yet telling myself I should have stayed behind. In my mind I told her that I loved her and missed her, and in my mind she forgave me as she sat beside my mother in the darkness and watched Sisak and me crawl faster and faster to the river.

I had lost all track of time when the ship's horn finally sounded. Oskina smiled then, as she would have if she had been beside me, and the river where I had left her was gone, and the thousand things I wanted to say to her had all been said. When the horn blew again I was on my feet, the sickness magically gone and my strength restored. I took a wedge of bread out of the bag and ate. I opened the jar of water and drank.

"Come on," I said.

"We can't go up yet," Gagik said.

But I was already out the door. I ran up the stairs to the deck.

Beyond the masts of a cluster of small boats, through a pale haze of fog, the city of Constantinople rose in dense tiers of domes and minarets and spires. Ships of all shapes and sizes bobbed in the blue-green water of its harbor, and the highest, longest bridge I had ever seen spanned its waterway. At the height of the city stood a blind stone monolith that could only be a fortress or a palace or a cathedral.

Gagik was standing beside me now, but neither of us said a word. There was nothing to say. Here was a city or a kingdom more impressive than any words we could use to describe it, and I could easily believe that the fountains of such a city were filled with gold and that the lights of such a city could turn night into day. Anything would be possible in such a city.

As we passed under the bridge, the realization that it was over, that I was safe at last, soared inside me, and at almost that exact moment I became aware that the ship had slowed, was stopping. In the middle distance between the ship and the brown line of the shore, I saw a small boat motoring toward us. I watched it casually at first, but as it drew closer, the tip of its bow pointed directly at us, I began to feel uneasy. There must have been a hundred harmless purposes for such boats in these waters, but for some reason I feared the purpose of this one. I kept hoping it would veer off, but it came straight on until finally I could see the uniform of the sailor at the helm. Beside the sailor, incredibly, impossibly, was a gendarme! Seeing his scarlet collar patches and holstered gun, my new world vanished and I was back in Sanis, running through a maze of streets to the sound of gunfire. But here there was nowhere to run. He had come for us and we were caught. Helplessly, as though a current of electricity held me where I stood, I watched a rope ladder being dropped over the side of the ship. A man who I guessed was the captain said, "That's for you two."

I looked at him, dumbfounded.

"You paid to go to Constantinople," he said. "Well, this is Constantinople. And there's the ladder. Down you go."

"Please," I said imploringly, hoping he might intercede on our behalf. But he had seen too many of our kind to worry about two more.

We descended the ladder and stepped into the small boat. As the boat motored away, the gendarme asked to see our passports.

"We don't have any passports," I said.

"Do you have any money?"

Gagik reached into his pocket and pulled out several coins, which the gendarme took. "Take off your shoes," he said.

Gagik took off his shoes, and the gendarme removed a five-lira note from one and handed the shoes back.

"What about you?" he said.

I gave him the two coins in my pocket.

"That's all?"

"That's all I have," I said.

"Take off your shoes."

I did so, and he looked inside one, then the other.

The boat was approaching a dirt bank. Fifteen yards from the bank, the boat stopped.

"Good-bye," the gendarme said.

I did not understand. Did he mean get out? Did he mean we were free, or was this what he always said before he shot someone? I looked at Gagik, who seemed to be frozen with fear.

"Get into the water!" the gendarme shouted.

Gagik stood and quickly stepped out of the boat. Instinctively, absurdly, I began to roll up my trousers.

"Out!" the gendarme said.

I stepped into the cool, waist-high water, not knowing if I would be shot in the back.

The boat began to motor away.

I looked at Gagik, then at the dirt bank. There were no soldiers or gendarmes waiting to arrest us;

there were no boats coming toward us. We seemed to be free.

I exhaled for what seemed like the first time in ten minutes and made a sound that was half laugh, half sigh. I turned to Gagik, who held out his trembling hands for me to see.

"I thought we were dead," he said. "Look at my hands. Mother of Jesus, I thought we were dead."

We started toward the bank. When my foot touched it, I dropped to my knees and thanked God, then picked up a handful of dirt, of freedom, and rubbed it on my arms and hands. I looked back at the sea, at the blue-green water and the cargo ship that distance had made small. I looked at the horizon beyond the sea, at a world I would never see again.

Chapter Thirty-four

We climbed a steep embankment to an elevated walkway that overlooked the sea and the boats in the harbor. The walkway was crowded with pedestrians, and the boulevard that ran alongside it was wider than any four streets I had ever seen. We crossed the boulevard and were moving with a crowd of a hundred or more up a cobbled street, the center of which was congested with carts and motorcars and horses and wagons and more people than we had ever seen in one place, speaking every language, it seemed, but our own. On either side were vendors and merchants of gold and silk and copper and spice, of tobacco and grain and silver and leather; mules burdened with blankets, and strolling peddlers calling out their wares: "Come here!" "You, boy!" "Come here. Come here." Above the street stood the gray-stained fronts of countless buildings whose tile roofs blocked the sun, and everywhere the smell of meat and bread mingled with the faint smell of the sea.

We were walking as quickly and as purposefully as our fellow pedestrians, and I felt, with Gagik beside me, like an army of two that had lost all the battles and still won the war. I walked with my family inside me, with their smiles on my lips, their relief in my heart. And I looked about myself at this new world with the eyes of the boy I had been and the man I felt myself to be.

We were nearing the top of the street when I stopped. Two men standing under the awning of a bookstore were speaking Armenian. It had been three years since I'd seen Armenians talking in the open, unafraid. Gagik and I listened for a moment, and one of the men looked at us, at our beggars' clothing and unwashed faces.

"What is it?" he said, assuming, I suppose, that we were going to ask him for money.

I told the man who I was and where I came from. I told him that my friend and I knew no one in Constantinople and that we had no place to stay and needed help. "Could you please help us?" I said.

"You said your name is Kenderian?"

"Yes."

"What is your father's name?"

"Sarkis."

"Your father is Sarkis Kenderian?"

"Yes," I said.

"I come from Bitlis myself. My name is Aram Nalbandian. What are you doing in Constantinople?"

I told him, and his face changed, and he began to shake his head. "Your family is dead, too?" he said to Gagik.

Gagik nodded.

The man shook his head and said a curse word quietly, to himself.

"Come with me," he said.

That was all he said. But looking back at the speed with which the following events occurred, those three words proved to be as magical an incantation as "Open Sesame." At that moment, time seemed to hand Gagik and me to our destiny, and the ground beneath our feet became a river carrying us to our new life. In a moment, we were standing before a three-story brick building that said JHAMANAK. On one of the windows was printed THE LEADING ARMENIAN NEWSPAPER IN CONSTANTINOPLE. Somewhere on that same window there should have been a sign that said GATEWAY TO THE TWENTIETH CENTURY, for when we stepped into the building, we also stepped into a new world of switchboards, ringing telephones, chattering typewriters, and working women, some of whom were smoking cigarettes and many of whom wore lipstick.

We were led past countless rows of desks, through a low, swinging door to the office of a Mr. Havian. Mr. Havian took us to the office of Mr. Charents. Mr. Charents listened to our stories and asked us if we were hungry.

We were.

Mr. Charents pushed a button on a black box and told the box to go to a certain restaurant and order every other item on the menu.

The box was silent.

Mr. Charents turned to Gagik and me. "Do you boys want dessert?"

We did.

"And dessert," Mr. Charents said to the black box.

"Yes, sir," the box said, and an hour later the trays of hot and cold food began to arrive—and arrive, until every desk, table, and chair in the room held at least one tray. Gagik and I ate until our stomachs were tight, and then we ate a little more.

And the river swept on. In a matter of minutes, we were in the backseat of an automobile taking us to St. Gregory's Orphanage. We were shaking hands with Mr. Nazarian, the director of the orphanage. We bathed and were given clean uniforms to wear—clean socks and underwear and new shoes. We were given a room with our own beds and pillows. And then we were saying good-bye to Mr. Nalbandian and Mr. Charents, we were shaking their hands and thanking them for all they had done, for everything.

And then the current of the river began to slow; and that night, when we finally got into our beds and lay our heads on our new pillows, it handed us back to time and disappeared beneath us.

Chapter Thirty-five

The war ended. Turkey and Germany had been defeated.

NEWS REPORTS

The triumvirate of Turkish leaders, Enver Pasha, Talaat Bey, and Djemal Pasha have fled the country.
Enver Pasha and Talaat Bey are said to be in Berlin,
reportedly with large sums of money expropriated
from their Armenian victims.

Eighty thousand Armenians were slain in Dorgor,
Arabia, alone. In the same region, seven thousand
children between the ages of three and ten years old
died of starvation.

The Turkish Parliament is dissolved. A newly
formed government has decided to create a general
court-martial for all functionaries responsible for the
massacre of Armenians.

My name is Vahan Kenderian. In 1918 I was fifteen
years old, the oldest boy at St. Gregory's Orphanage in

Constantinople. Three years before, I had been a member of one of the richest and most influential families in Turkey. I had been a reflection of a safe and privileged world, and beneath me was a net as wide as my father's influence, as strong as my mother's love. Now I was only one of two hundred fifty orphans, and my future was nothing more than a white canvas, a block of marble, a lump of clay.

I had lost three years of schooling, and I was determined to learn as much as I could. The more I learned, I reasoned, the more I could become—for myself and my family. Every morning, I awakened in a bed beside four other beds, and it was the steel inside me that made it possible for me to get out of that bed and pretend I was myself; it was the steel that helped me study when all the other boys had gone to sleep.

In four months I completed the entire curriculum for the year.

NEWS REPORTS

Turkish trials begin in Constantinople. Kemal Bey, the governor of Diarbekir, is the first to be tried for his participation in the Armenian massacres in the Yozghad district.

Reshid Bey, the former governor of Diarbekir

---

and one of the enforcers of the Armenian butcheries, kills himself when he is caught by police.

Kemal Bey, the governor of Diarbekir, is found guilty of crimes against the Armenians and publicly hanged in Bayazid Square in Stamboul.

Throughout Asia Minor, Armenians are still being persecuted by the Turks. The fact that the Armistice has been signed seems to make no difference.

On the recommendation of Father Ohanian, who later joined a committee to reunite Armenian families separated by the holocaust, I was admitted to St. Mesrop's School for Boys. Every day I took a streetcar to my new school, and every night I returned to the orphanage. When I closed my eyes at night, I felt a hollowness inside me that nothing could fill. Somewhere inside me I knew that my grandmother still lay by the bank of the River Tigris, that the bones of my father still lay on the road to Diarbekir. I knew that the home I had lost represented a million other homes, and the city I had lost represented the nation of what had once been Armenia. I knew that there would never again be another Bitlis or Erzerum or Van, that the world I had known would survive only in the seed I carried within me, and that the memories of that seed would fade as one generation succeeded another. I knew that I was free, and that I would never be free.

One night I dreamed about my mother. We were standing on opposite banks of a river. I called to her, but she could not hear me above the sound of the water. I waved her toward me, but she shook her head; she could not come.

NEWS REPORTS

The British government, which has arrested and detained many Young Turk officials on the island of Malta, has been persuaded to release the perpetrators of genocide in exchange for British soldiers captured by Turkish Nationalist forces.

Talaat Bey is assassinated in a Berlin suburb by an Armenian student.

Djemal Pasha is assassinated in Tiflis by two Armenians.

Enver Pasha, the last of the Young Turk triumvirate responsible for the genocide, is killed in Tarkestan fighting in the Bashmachi revolt against Russia.

Estimates reveal that nearly three-quarters of the Armenian population of Turkey, one million five

hundred thousand men, women, and children, has
perished.

Once a week I took a streetcar to the Armenian ceme-
tery four miles from St. Gregory's Orphanage. I felt at
home among those graves, as though I were standing in
the center of my own heart, within the gated perimeter
of a longing that would never age, never end, never
grow wise. Here was Sisak, and my mother and father,
my grandmother and Diran and Tavel, Seta and Armenouhi and Oskina. These were their graves, and I spoke
to them soundlessly, from the deepest part of myself. I
planted flowers beside their graves, and I picked the
weeds that grew between the flowers and felt the air
weighted by a sublime and compassionate presence.

I have learned this about life: I know, as my neighbors
in Bitlis tried to tell me, that there is pain and disillusion in the heart of it. I know, as my father knew, that
character and discipline are the steel that fortify it, and
that somewhere, beyond pain and disillusion, great
blessings are made.

EPILOGUE

On September 4, 1920, Vahan and Oskina Kenderian were reunited by Father Ohanian outside the church of St. Gregory's Orphanage. Their names are among those of four hundred other Armenians who arrived at Ellis Island in May 1921 to begin new lives in the United States.

They never saw their mother or uncle again. Meera Kenderian died of cholera five days after her two remaining sons escaped. Their uncle Mumpreh was killed with three other Armenians, fighting Turkish soldiers from an abandoned house in Bitlis.

THE END

This book is for Vahridj Kenderian,
whose story I was honored to tell.

This book is for my mother,
who gave me the key.